Lisette Sheen
26/04/25

THE MANSE

MARIA'S MYSTERY

LISETTE SKEET

Strategic Book Publishing and Rights Co.

Strategic Book Publishing and Rights Co., LLC
USA | Singapore
www.sbpra.net

For information about special discounts for bulk purchases, please contact Strategic Book Publishing and Rights Co., LLC Special Sales, at bookorder@sbpra.net.

ISBN: 978-1-68235-698-2

They are not long, the days of wine and roses:
Out of a misty dream
Our path emerges for a while, then closes
Within a dream.

Ernest Dowson (1867–1900)

This story is a work of fiction.
Characters are not the same as anyone who exists, although accidental similarities may occur.

CONTENTS

Introduction

There is something about a genuinely peaceable, good-natured woman that causes a certain type of person to imagine they may walk all over her. This likelihood increases if she happens to be naturally pretty. Men may feel certain that they can be the stronger force in a relationship. In terms of other women, admiring friends may be genuine but, when envy creeps in, the temptation to be manipulative seems even greater.

Being very feminine and naturally pretty (so pretty that others lose their reason) isn't every woman's good fortune. For those who do possess those charms, life can bring some powerful, often unexpected experiences. They may encounter events which affect them in a way that others never experience. However, this may not always feel advantageous.

When others respond according to appearances and their own perceptions, their behaviour may be challenging. Women who possess true beauty may find themselves bullied because of it. The root cause is often jealousy, and an insecure partner, or friend, or colleague will seek to gain control. In a relationship, a pretty woman may be perceived as weak; however, an apparent softness coupled with an adorable appearance doesn't guarantee that she is easily led, and those who try to act on their assumptions may find themselves confounded by her strength of character. They respond angrily,

1

when they realise their mistake.

For Maria, friendships, romantic relationships and even casual acquaintances can be problematic. Men, irresistibly attracted by her slim figure, plait of golden-brown hair and long-lashed grey-green eyes, find themselves challenged by her determination and high achieving qualities. When she shows how well-equipped she is to conduct her life independently, they become dissatisfied.

Maria has a compassionate nature but she is much tougher than she appears. Dynamic and unequivocal, she prefers to make her own decisions and shows strength and resilience when challenged. Having left behind a set of difficulties caused by other people in first one, then another workplace, Maria keeps her strength of character and goes further this time. She is determined that she will be true to herself.

CHALLENGES

Maria's golden-brown hair fell to her waist and she wore it in a heavy braid. Freckles on her creamy English skin framed her lips and smothered her cheeks and brow to her hairline.

A young woman of slender build, nevertheless she possessed considerable strength, being a competent horsewoman and a trained groom. She enjoyed being active and was well-equipped to care for horses in a world she loved.

The manager of the racing stables, where she was employed for some months, was attracted to Maria. He knew her skills; their interests were similar and they began to spend time together. Jason seemed proud to be in Maria's company, especially whenever they went out to dinner or to socialise with others. He was a good-looking man and she responded to his efforts to win her interest; however, when she found herself being drawn into a relationship, it was not long before she had qualms, because he was very high-handed.

Just a few months passed before emotions began to be fraught with disagreement. Jason was fair-haired and immaculate, the kind of man who turned heads. The only son of wealthy, indulgent parents, he was also well used to getting his own way. In the company of women, he believed in his entitlement to flirt freely despite having a girlfriend; yet he became annoyed if he perceived interest in

Maria from other men. When this happened, he seemed to view their attentions as the result of her deliberate efforts.

Maria was naturally beautiful. Since approaches from fascinated males happened often, she had learnt to deal with them competently and it was not pleasant to be mistrusted. As time passed and the uncomfortable feeling of being watched for wrongdoing grew stronger, she knew it was unnecessary to allow herself to be controlled by her partner. Jason wanted Maria to be acquiescent all the time, but her character was too strong. Petty arguments continually arose over minor episodes that were not her fault, and she decided not to tolerate his behaviour. She ended the relationship and left him, with his angry words ringing in her ears.

"You're too frivolous, you're too careless! You don't know what men are like!"

She also, therefore, left the job, which would have been uncomfortable to maintain after that because Jason was sullen.

For a time, her main employment became office work.

* * *

On the first day of her new job in the administrative department of a community college, Maria entered the office wearing a neat fawn suit, smart brown court shoes and a pale pink scarf tucked into her collar. She seated herself at her desk and turned on a computer. Waiting for the screen to open, she sat back in her chair, putting up a hand to tuck a wisp of hair behind her ear. She looked around her. The room was very quiet. A young man was standing at a photocopying machine but he ignored Maria. She began to unpack a collection of pens and pencils. A small woman dressed in dark trousers and a crisp, white shirt, appeared at her elbow.

The woman didn't introduce herself. Without preamble, she asked a question. "Are you staying?"

Maria had a modest bag, which she kept close to her on a shoulder strap. She wondered if it made her look as if she was about to leave, but decided the question needed no answer. With a smile and a nod, she continued to sort her things into pencil holders and assumed the woman would wander off. Instead, the sentence was repeated more loudly.

Maria looked up at the small person's face and saw an aggressive stare. Surprised, she was silent for a moment, then she answered the question. "Yes, of course I'm staying! I have a bag handy, with a few sweets in case of low blood sugar. I don't want a headache to spoil my day. Most of us have a few essentials which we carry around, I suppose?"

She stopped speaking, feeling annoyed with herself for finding excuses for something that was not the other woman's business!

"It makes you look as if you're not staying!"

The woman wanted her to remove the bag from her arm. They were not in a front office where, just possibly, her appearance might look too casual, thought Maria. Yet, why would it? Her bag was neat and her scarf was barely visible above a smart jacket; her hair was plaited as usual and pinned in a coil at her neck, and she was made-up. It seemed best to end this confrontation. Maria slipped the strap from her shoulder, pulled at her scarf to loosen it and hastily stowed her possessions into the top drawer of the desk. She was uncomfortably aware of a continued cold gaze, but now it was aimed at the glossy varnish she wore on her nails.

Maria was so irritated by the intrusive woman, whose name turned out to be Phyllis, she was tempted to jump up from her desk and leave. Instead, on a deep breath, she began to work, found she enjoyed it, and soon thought she could put the incident behind her.

A pleasant female boss was quite different from Phyllis. Mild-mannered and non-judgemental, she was happy to hand over plenty of responsibility, which meant Maria's mind was fully occupied each day. She made a friend when she was introduced to the office receptionist, a good-natured older lady named Sheila, who had worked within the college for many years.

Sheila wore her bleached hair short and sprayed hard with lacquer. She chose simple skirts and jumpers in subdued colours and did not, it seemed, get herself the wrong side of the envious Phyllis by adding pretty accessories to her outfits. She liked Maria, and occasionally they ate their lunch together in a nearby bistro, where they enjoyed friendly conversations over wedges of hot quiche accompanied by a good deal of salad for Sheila, who said she had a weight problem.

Disappointingly, it became obvious to everyone in the office that Phyllis was on a mission to upset Maria. It was comforting to know she had sympathetic interest from the others, but gossiping about a colleague during coffee breaks was not Maria's style. She had begun to understand that the woman would encroach on her personal space at the slightest opportunity. The behaviour was embarrassing. At last, when Phyllis brought a sheaf of papers to Maria's desk one day and saw fit to lean on the back of her chair with the *front* of her body, hip-thrusting, Maria wouldn't tolerate it. She handed in her notice.

Maria was not someone who bothered to prevaricate if an environment could damage her wellbeing. Like the episode with Jason, her femininity and strength posed challenges, probably imaginary but for a certain type of person, hard to bear. Phyllis had a powerful wish to be controlling but, even if she had possessed charisma, she had no hope of forcing Maria into her idea of a mould, even for a few months. In another strand of the awkward situation which was also comparable to Maria's experience with Jason, it seemed this person sensed Maria's composed and attractive exterior masked a certain strength of character and the fact made her combative. Ultimately, it was a trait she underestimated.

Sheila was disappointed when her new friend decided to leave but she admitted that she definitely saw the reason why. The two women shared a last drink after work and over glasses of red wine they got a little emotional. Maria realised, with Sheila's affectionate agreement, there must have been some envy affecting poor Phyllis.

"She's never owned a cute handbag!" Sheila said.

"Do you think she'd want one?"

"No. I think she's a bit messed up by your presence, Maria!"

With her close-cropped hair, belted trousers and heavy footwear, Phyllis was absolutely entitled to express herself as the person she was. Yet, it was clear that she thought Maria's womanly appearance affected her, somehow. Perhaps her responses went deeper than she, herself, understood? Not only did she feel annoyed but she was also fascinated by the more feminine woman. It didn't matter to Maria but she promised to keep in touch with Sheila.

* * *

Maria's parents lived in the family home deep in the Suffolk countryside, where she and her brother and sister were brought up. They had decided to go abroad at Christmas, and treat themselves to a sunny holiday instead of staying in England for the festivities. It was a long time since Maria and her siblings were children but she felt a little forlorn after her mother told her about the decision, although she knew she must make plans of her own.

She hunted for something she could do, that would enable her to look after animals and to leave her home town for the Christmas period. She found an advertisement online and it looked very interesting. An elderly gentleman needed a responsible, experienced groom to care for horses and dogs for a few weeks, from the start of December until soon after the New Year. His regular horseman would be taking a break. The new employee would not be suitable if they feared large dogs; one was a Rhodesian Ridgeback.

The address of the estate began *the Manse*; there was a photograph of a stately mansion set in vast grounds and (in a deciding factor for Maria) a picture of two handsome hunters; one chestnut, the other bay.

Maria applied for the groom's position and was accepted almost at once. Looking forward to abandoning her make-up and suits in a return to her most familiar and beloved work, she felt excited and began to plan and prepare her luggage well before it would be needed. Meanwhile, she took a temporary job, standing in for a hotel receptionist for the last weeks of summer. She would travel to the Welsh border at the very end of November.

The Manse

Passing through the open gates of the great house, Maria's taxi was driven slowly along a broad driveway. The route wound through parkland for a quarter of a mile before finally opening out in a sweep of gravel, where the car came to a halt at the front of the property.

The building, which had stood there for almost three hundred years, was once the home of the local vicar. It was very beautiful, built of grey stone and with high, mullioned windows. The walls were smothered in ivy.

The afternoon was peaceful. Rooks could be heard cawing in tall trees, some distance away to the right and there was an intermittent sound of the bleating of sheep. Maria stood surrounded by her luggage, and with the crunch of wheels on gravel the driver turned the car and left her there in front of the great house. The still air was very cold; shivering despite her heavy coat, she slung a knapsack across her shoulders, tucked a handbag under one arm, picked up a case and carried everything towards a grand front doorway.

A plump lady wearing a flower-patterned apron bound firmly around her waist, admitted Maria. She said her name was Mrs Moss and mentioned, unsmiling, that staff usually entered by the door of a porch at the side.

"I'll remember," promised Maria, conscious that this advice was somewhat brusquely given and hoping at once that she was not about to face new problems. However, the woman relieved her of her knapsack and together they made their way up a broad staircase.

"Won't I sleep above the stables?" Maria was surprised, as she was shown into a bedroom high above the main rooms, on an upper floor. "There was a picture in the job description?"

Mrs Moss was somewhat out of breath but she said "Robert puts *stable rooms* in the advertisement, in case he gets a lad. The bedsit's alright for a boy but Robert wouldn't keep a girl out of the main house! You'll be here …"

Maria found herself in a spacious room, painted in cream-and-white. It was well supplied with bedroom furniture, including a double bed, a dressing table and a tall swing mirror, all in dark wood and gleaming with polish. There was a fitted, fawn-coloured carpet. A padded window-seat was tucked into the lower curves of one tall window. Books were stacked on a low table nearby. Behind the bedhead, wallpaper in an old gold shade embossed with paler velvet flowers lent a luxurious touch.

"Oh!" She was enchanted. "This is *lovely!*"

The older woman nodded and left her alone.

After a few minutes, dressed in a pair of neat trousers and a roll neck sweater, Maria returned to the lower floor of the mansion, where she would meet her new employer. Mrs Moss was waiting at the foot of the stairs, to lead her across the polished floor and faded mats in the hallway to a sitting-room, where an old gentleman was sitting near a crackling log fire. He stood up as Maria approached, and held out his right hand in welcome.

"Here's your lass!" declared the housekeeper, before withdrawing from the room.

Robert was a retired doctor and psychotherapist, and the Manse was his home. The property and much surrounding land belonged to him. Aged nearly eighty, he was very tall, and he looked truly in keeping with his surroundings in his country tweeds. His outfit was adorned with a silk tie in a bright shade of green.

Maria would learn that he wrote learned volumes which reflected his experiences in general practice and afterwards when he saw clients privately for psychoanalysis. As an author he could work when he felt alert, and rest when the inevitable problems of old age threatened to hold him back.

Robert had always led a privileged life but he was deeply conscious that he enjoyed good fortune and he was a compassionate man.

With an apologetic air, the elderly gentleman informed his new employee that she would need to begin to care for his hunters that same day.

"As well as these two devils!" He pulled open one half of tall French windows, just wide enough to admit from the garden two excited dogs. They were an English Springer Spaniel and a Rhodesian Ridgeback. They rushed in eagerly, with wagging tails and tremendous friendliness. "They can be quite boisterous!"

He meant to warn Maria but the dogs had already cannoned into her knees. Maria learnt their names were Boy and Jaff. She was glad to see that Boy, the spaniel, had an undocked tail but she was reminded of some previous employers, where wealthy families indulged their love of dogs but without paying attention to the animals' training. However, she was well used to dogs. Feeling thankful that they weren't muddy, she patted them, deliberately adopting a calm air so that she didn't give the pair any ideas that she would get involved with a rough game. This, their owner observed and nodded approvingly.

"That's right," he commented. "They won't make pests of themselves if you don't encourage their nonsense!"

Robert was obviously a kindly man. He asked Maria if her room was satisfactory and made sure she knew that if anything concerned or worried her, she was to let him know. He described the dogs' daily needs but was brief on the subject of the horses, since he said she would meet them in the stables and with the experience she detailed in her application, no doubt she would know what to do for them. Their feeding charts, he thought, were "on the wall in there". The groom was heading away on a long-planned trip to visit relatives in Australia, and he had already left much earlier in the day. The horses were called Ed and Cass, said Robert; she would see the brass name plates fixed to their stable doors. After a pause, he observed that Ed was the livelier of the two.

Maria smiled. She suspected this meant that Ed was a handful to ride, but she emphasised that she was competent and the horses would both be safe. They agreed that she could return with any questions if she needed to.

After that, with the dogs at her heels she left Robert and went out-of-doors via the porch which Mrs Moss had indicated, then made her way across the gravel driveway into the yard, where she approached the stable building and entered. Two horses turned intelligent faces to watch, as she approached the stalls. A chestnut hunter of mighty size and a bright, bay hunter just a hand or so smaller: they were Cass and Ed.

* * *

Maria was experienced in working in well-run riding stables, as well as racing establishments. She had never entered a tack room that was not kept in good order. Exploring, she expected to be assailed by the smell of clean leather, shining with the application of saddle soap. Metal bits, buckles and stirrup irons should gleam (she was taught when she trained). Harness must be supple from regular care.

From the heavy bundle of keys given to her, it was easy to select the one labelled with a twisted tag and pencilled scrawl *Tack Room* but the door opened stiffly, the hinges creaked and the interior of the lean-to shed had a musty odour that was immediately apparent. She flicked a switch on the wall to her right and an unshaded bulb produced a dim light which revealed cobwebs in corners and dust on a row of saddles. She could tell which of the saddles had been used most recently but they were far from spotless. She longed to clean up and make the place look as it should.

* * *

Working for a part of each morning following her rides, Maria made changes. There was a butler sink and a tap, which turned stiffly but clean, cold water shot from it and could be used. A couple of battered tin mugs looked too old to drink from but she filled them with water and sluiced the stone floor of the tack room before sweeping it thoroughly to get rid of every bit of mud and dirt that lay there. Beneath the sink, the discovery of a packet of unused blue cloths was like coming upon a small treasure trove.

She opened and scrubbed two small windows, letting in fresh air to dry the floor and freshen the room until the winter's chill became too much to bear. She dusted and wiped shelves, finding old tins of coffee alongside packets of solidified granulated sugar. Everything had dried out long ago and she threw it all away.

A small gas ring worked and burned with a strong blue flame when lit but the surfaces around it bore a litter of used teabags and spilt sugar. Maria disposed of the rubbish, boiled water in a small kettle, used the dregs of some washing-up liquid from a plastic bottle found beneath the sink, and washed the enamel hob.

Boy and Jaff were constantly at Maria's heels and it didn't take more than one foray into the tack room before they jostled one another to follow her. A small, electric heater had been stowed beneath the long counter that ran along one wall; she dragged it out to examine and found it had surely been used quite recently, since there were fingerprints around the switches and a layer of dust only covered its top. The plug was new. With doors and windows closed, the fire was turned on and the dogs soon understood that this was a source of blissful warmth. Maria found a pile of thick saddle cloths, which she shook out before throwing them down on the stone floor for the animals. They settled themselves there and kept her company while she thoroughly washed, dried and polished the neglected leather and brass.

When Maria had an opportunity to visit the village, she made her way there on foot, finding the route was straightforward and not a great distance. The walk took her downhill, via lanes and beside hedgerows, until the modest collection of houses and a main road opened before her. A grocery store was prominent, with a blue-and-white striped awning over a front window and wooden tubs full of fruit and vegetables stacked by the door. Supplies of teabags, instant coffee granules, sugar, dried milk and chocolate biscuits were purchased, along with a pair of smart, white mugs made of the resilient material used for camping supplies. She bought a light bulb, several plastic containers and a packet of plastic spoons.

Upon her return, Maria stowed her tea-making equipment inside the containers, snapped lids on tightly and placed them on the newly-clean shelves of her den.

The tack room became a cosy sanctuary which was especially comforting to enter after an hour's ride in the cold, December air. Full of familiar scents like saddle soap and coffee, it could be made very warm with the little heater. Since the dogs accompanied Maria often when she worked in the stables and around the yard, they added to her growing feeling of being very much at home.

* * *

There was no evidence of neglect inside the Manse, where the grand hallway was graced with tall vases loaded with dried flowers, ferns and berries. Several times over the course of each month, two women came to work there for a whole day, keeping the rooms clean and cared for. A taxi driver who owned a small local business was responsible for collecting them from the village a few miles away and taking them home again later. Towards the end of the year, their routine altered and during one week just ahead of December they were there every morning, making the mansion scrupulously clean and ready for the festivities. Then, leaving well-swept carpets, polished surfaces and scents of lavender and vanilla lingering in the air, they were given time off until New Year and general tidying and upkeep were the responsibilities of Mrs Moss. As a result of the ladies' efforts everything looked very good when Maria arrived.

In the kitchen, crystal tiles covered floors throughout the working space, the pantry, a utility room and surrounding the ovens. The cleaners ensured the tiles were swept and washed. Everything was ordered as Mrs Moss preferred it. She kept the cupboards well stocked and work surfaces gleaming with cleanliness. If this zeal occasionally made things difficult for Robert, who was apt to fancy a sandwich during the evening and potter about by himself, choosing ingredients and preparing a tray, he did not complain. Certainly, he could find everything he needed but the risk of running into trouble for making a mess was always there! When Mrs Moss returned in the morning, she always seemed to know about his latest foray into her domain and she would serve his coffee with a grumble to the effect that he had not replaced a pickle jar exactly where it should be, or covered the cheese in the refrigerator. However, her short patience was counter-balanced by efficiency and Robert put up with her.

Robert's grandson, Ian, lived in the mansion and his rooms were near the very top of the old building. At first, Maria thought she would see him only rarely, since he seemed to have a well-ordered routine which included time alone in his small private study most mornings. Maria passed this room on her way downstairs; the door was often ajar and she saw his back view, bent over his desk.

Sometimes, he spent an hour in a private gymnasium where equipment including a rowing machine, a cross trainer and weights was arranged in a long room situated on the ground floor.

At around mid-day he usually went out in the type of heavy-duty vehicle which is designed to withstand muddy and stony routes, heading away, across the tracks that bordered parkland and led to fields and crofts beyond.

* * *

There came a heavy rainfall, in a torrent that began early on a cold, grey morning and continued all that day and into the night until, by the second afternoon it seemed never-ending.

The hunters were not young but they had been tended well, and they were full of intelligent interest in the humans who took care of their many needs. Daily exercise was essential. Often, Maria saddled one horse to ride out and put a headcollar and leading rein on the other, to bring alongside. She headed across the parkland during the first days of her stay but with the rain there would be a big issue with mud along the tracks and field edges.

She hunted through the set of keys, found one labelled *Manege* and unlocked the doors to the broad building which was the indoor school. There was dust on the door handles, along the top of a low wall around the schooling space and in all the crevices, but wood chips were still thickly spread on the floor. When she led Cass inside, he raised his head and looked around as if he might be as appreciative of a dry place to exercise as Maria herself.

Cass was seventeen hands high and Maria used the mounting block in the stable yard before a hack. Inside the school, she hopped up onto his back via the surrounding interior wall. She began to circle the school, letting the horse walk on a loose rein, stretching his neck. Maria had memories of learning to ride when she was very young, when she was often forced to share just an hour-long lesson with several other riders, being chastised by a short-tempered tutor. Now, gathering up the reins and sending her mount into an extended trot, she could manage her session exactly as she wished. Great mirrors lined an end wall but Maria's riding lessons were long past. She glanced briefly at her reflection, then urged Cass forward into a lively walk to warm him up before sending him into a trot.

His hoofbeats thudded over the ground. They described circles, crossing the school diagonally to change the rein.

Maria thoroughly enjoyed the ride but Cass was happy too. There was so much space to use and at last it tempted them and they skidded faster, out of a beautiful, balanced canter into a mad dash they both fully intended, before finally slowing to a gentle walk again.

There was a sound of clapping.

"What ...?" Maria looked around and saw Ian, who had opened the gate into the manege and was sitting on the wall to watch her ride.

She turned the horse to face him, unable to resist a little flourish of expertise, making Cass walk a few paces backwards as if in deference to his usual master. Cass obeyed and then she halted him. He shook his head, mouthing the bit.

"Well!" Ian crossed the arena to pat Cass but the horse was excited. He nodded his head up and down, making it impossible to stroke him. Ian stood back, looking up at Maria. "You aren't just a pretty face, are you?" He grinned up at her. "I hope that didn't sound rude! Honestly, it was good to see old Cass trying his best like that."

"No ..." Maria dismounted, landing easily on the soft ground. "I didn't mind."

She turned her attention to loosening the girth, and Ian went automatically around to the opposite side of the horse, to run up a stirrup iron.

"Ed is the nuttier horse ..." Ian remarked as they walked out of the schooling area. The sound of the horse's hoofbeats changed as they crossed the concrete in the yard.

"I know!" Maria had already found Ed a lively ride. "But I wouldn't have taken a job like this unless I could cope!"

Having brought her ride to an end a little abruptly, she began to walk the horse around in a circle at a slow pace.

"Point taken," Ian agreed. "Clearly, you can!"

GUESTS

The dogs were given their food in the kitchen and it was Maria's responsibility to make sure they received the quantities Robert stipulated. She mixed tinned dog food with plain biscuits and added a pill for the spaniel to guard against occasional troublesome pains in his joints. While they waited for Maria to prepare their bowls, Boy and Jaff knew how to behave and they watched her with dark brown and amber eyes respectively, sitting side by side, looking like the best dogs anyone could wish for.

To begin with, if he crossed her path Ian had acknowledged Maria in passing with a nod or a cool, murmured *good morning*. He became more friendly after they chatted in the manege. He wandered into the kitchen while this process was going on, saw that Maria had used the last scrapings from a tin and reached for a new one from a high cupboard. He opened it. They could hear the landline in the house ringing, and Robert's voice when he answered the call. Maria was aware that Robert replaced the receiver and went into a small study off the lower corridor to talk privately.

The dogs had finished their food and Maria was washing cutlery at the sink, when Robert entered the kitchen.

"Sally called from the pub," he said. "She has two refugees from the storm. The river in front of their house is flooded and they can't get through it to go home. There were problems for some others ahead of these two and now there are no rooms available at the Two Pigeons, so I've agreed to let them come here!"

"What kind of refugees?" Ian was leaning against a counter where he had been drinking coffee and watching rain lashing at the window. The sky was dark. Maria saw him turn his attention to his grandfather. She stepped past him to close the curtains, thinking his question sounded cautious.

"Human ones," said Robert, shortly. He would not engage in a debate; he had made a decision and it was his right, of course, to do so. He opened a wall cupboard to find a coffee cup, and helped himself from the cafetiere.

* * *

In fact, the young woman who arrived at around seven o'clock that evening was unassuming and so grateful to find a safe place to stay, it would have been churlish for Ian to create an argument. Amelia clambered from Sally's car looking white-faced and tired. She approached the mansion with her arm around the shoulders of a small boy. She explained that she lived with her young son in cottage on the far side of the village but for now there was no hope of crossing the river, as the bridge was under water. Fortunately, she had no pets to worry about and the house was safely locked up.

Robert treated the new arrivals with typical courtesy. He welcomed them and emphasised that they were not to feel concerned about the length of their stay. On the contrary, he insisted, it was very nice to have guests. However, it was obvious that the pair looked shy. He did not expect them to keep him company that evening and instead, suggested they warm themselves by the kitchen Aga, where no doubt Mrs. Moss would ensure they were provided with tea. This, they did, finding comfort, as well as a diversion in the enthusiastic attentions of the dogs.

Mrs Moss made tea and permitted Maria to open a packet of chocolate biscuits. After washing the teacups with some excessive crashing about at the sink, she became somewhat curt and went home earlier than usual. Maria was unworried. She would take on the task of making the evening meal, and once this decision was made, she enjoyed gathering ingredients together, planning a simple meal for herself, Robert and Ian. She selected a giant pan and emptied two large cans of tomatoes into it, along with chopped celery, garlic, seasonings and some water. She would warm rolls in the oven and serve them along with bowls of hot soup with grated cheese for a topping. There would be enough food for Amelia and Peter, she thought, if indeed they needed to stay.

As the sound of heavy rain against the windows reminded everyone of the floods in the village, the new guests had no option but to accept Robert's kind offer of further hospitality and he readily assured them of their continued welcome.

Maria served her home-made soup to Robert and Ian, who sat at the dining table in a room adjacent to the long sitting room, as was their custom. Sharing wine, they were chatting with one another but made sure to thank Maria when she took in the meal. They were fully appreciative of her efforts. She filled a basket with crisp, warm bread rolls and took them to the table along with a dish of grated cheese, and also, a fresh green salad. When she noticed little Peter watching her with great eyes, she gave him a small task and he proudly took a silver butter dish into the dining room, and was thanked just as graciously.

It was inevitable that, as newcomers to the household, Amelia and her son were feeling lost and both were clearly very tired. Maria suggested a relaxing bath for Amelia so, supplied with a mug full of soup, she obediently went upstairs, leaving Peter in a cosy nest of cushions on the old chair by the stove.

Maria remembered something. She disliked soup when she was very young. Thinking Peter might feel the same, she made a milky drink, filled a roll with cheese and kept the child company while he ate and finished the supper. He began to fall asleep, resting a flushed cheek against his mother's jacket on the chair arm.

Amelia looked more relaxed after her bath and time to herself. She helped to clear crockery and would have dried it but Maria suggested she might rest in the sitting room instead, and soon she fell asleep in a corner of the sofa, looking childlike herself. Maria went upstairs, delved into the vast airing cupboard beside Ian's room and found a rug, which she took to cover the younger woman's shoulders.

The evening wore on. Robert watched a television documentary. Ian appeared in the sitting room, with a sleeping bag slung over his shoulder. Thankfully he was being good-natured about lending his own room that night. It was selected by Robert for their visitors since it had been in recent use and it would feel warm. Ian had mildly protested at first, saying that the mansion had plenty of space but there was no malice in his words. He understood his grandfather's wish to make the young mother and her son as comfortable as possible and radiators had been keeping his suite cosy ever since the weather became cold.

So, for one night, Ian's bedroom and en suite bathroom were commandeered. Amelia would sleep in a second single bed which was always kept there, and Peter would have a folding divan, placed beside her.

Prior to her departure, Mrs Moss had stripped Ian's own bed, covered its mattress with clean ticking and a coverlet, and pushed it against a far wall. From the airing cupboard, she had collected pillows, fresh sheets and blankets; these, she piled on an easy chair which stood near the tall bedroom window in readiness for making up two beds for the young mother and her son.

Before long, it was Maria who checked the temperature of the room and made up the spare single bed and small divan, ensuring they were placed side-by-side so that Peter would feel safe near his mother. To be absolutely sure of their warmth, she dug into the back of the vast airing cupboard and found extra quilts to throw over the coverlets. She switched on a low lamp above the head of the single bed, turned off the harsher central light, and then ran downstairs to raid the library for a handful of story books, which she put on a shelf beneath the lamp. With the drapes covering the window, the stormy night was hidden. Everything, she decided, looked inviting.

She spoke to Amelia and woke her, then they encouraged Peter to walk upstairs, which he managed to do, albeit sleepily. Amelia helped him remove his trousers, then she tucked him into the divan bed, where he closed his eyes at once.

"Thank you!" she said to Maria, looking around her. "I'm so grateful for … all this!" Her relief and exhaustion were obvious.

"Well, it's Robert whom we have to thank," Maria told her. "He is so kind! He has made me very comfortable, too."

She said goodnight and left Amelia to rest and recover.

* * *

After such a flurry of activity, Maria was glad to sit quietly in the sitting room. Robert had made it clear that she was welcome to share the rooms with the family. The atmosphere was peaceful and the fire, supplied with a shovel full of coal, glowed red without its usual crackle of burning wood.

Ian wandered over to the drinks cabinet and poured a small brandy for himself. He offered to bring drinks for Maria and Robert but they were sharing a tray of tea and both declined the offer.

"I'm going to turn in. In my sleeping bag." Ian waited but if he had thoughts of saying more, his grandfather's expression stopped him. Robert peered over his spectacles with raised brows, saying nothing.

Was he trying to flirt? Joke about being lonely? Maria remained composed. Perhaps he was simply grumbling, mildly, that he was displaced! "Sleep well!" was all she said.

Ian accepted their implied reproofs. "Sorry!" he apologised, then took his sleeping bag and made for the cosy study on the ground floor. There, a small fire still blazed. He would settle himself on the sofa, Robert said, adding that he probably rather liked the idea of resting so comfortably, with books to hand if he decided to read before falling asleep later. There was a pause, then Robert went on, with a comment that seemed obtuse.

"You are strong enough to tell him off," he observed. "You should, if you need to … but let me know if you feel uncomfortable. He's thirty-four years old but he could do with growing up a bit!"

* * *

The next day, forgiving Ian for his cheek, Maria rode with him and they had fun, sharing a liking for a fast ride, finding fallen trees and low fences to jump. The ground remained damp following the storms of the day before, so they picked their route carefully, using the worn tracks around the fields.

After they had used up their own energies and those of their mounts, they returned to the yard at a walk, chatting amicably. Both the horses had seemed to enjoy being put through their paces.

Before parting, Maria and Ian cleaned the muddy tack together.

Maria plunged stirrup irons into soapy water. Their conversation resumed and she found herself telling Ian that her brother, who was a farm manager in Suffolk, had similar interests to his own.

"He enjoys the gym …" Her words tailed off. She was conscious of her attempt to place this lively, attractive man in a friendly, even brotherly role which (she hoped) he wouldn't think he could change.

"Uh huh," Ian continued to polish a saddle. He was unabashed. "Is your brother handsome, clever and a good chap?"

Maria laughed. "All of the above!" He had caught her out. "Oh! Enough!"

It was a watershed, in a way. Perhaps it was sufficient acknowledgement that Ian had begun to seem flirtatious; also, that Maria

knew it and wouldn't want it to go on. She thought he would aban-
don the idea and hoped they would remain comfortable in one
another's company.

Maria had to admit, just to herself, that she enjoyed their shared
rides. She could make Ian laugh and once she realised that, the
temptation was always there, although she was determined she did
not feel physically attracted to him. Nevertheless, there was nothing
to find fault with in the way he looked! So attractive, he was
immaculately clean-shaven with sparkling brown eyes, thick, dark
hair cropped very short, and a wide smile. He looked after his
health and she often heard the whir of gym equipment in the early
mornings, when she went downstairs to begin the horses' routine.
He was a young man who had good looks as well as a lively sense
of humour but, forcing herself to be honest, Maria thought she had
made enough mistakes in her life already. At the racing stables, she
remembered being aware that Jason was too high-handed, yet she
entered into a relationship with him without considering how he
might behave as a partner. Ian seemed to have a more affable character but there was no doubt that he, too, liked his own way.

* * *

When Amelia arrived at the Manse, there was a worried expression
in her almond-shaped blue eyes. A young woman of slim build, she
had small hands and feet. Her pale skin gave her an air of fragility,
and the fair hair pinned into a tight knot on top of her head did
nothing to relieve her tense appearance. With nervous gestures she
kept Peter close to her side, until Maria convinced her that she was
free to relax in a warm bath while the child was safely tucked into
an easy chair in the warm kitchen. Amelia couldn't hide her feelings;
she had been going through a tough time and was looking pale and
strained.

Hoping to make the poor girl feel better, very early the next day,
Maria inspected empty rooms in the house. She liked caring for

people almost as much as she enjoyed looking after horses! After rejecting a couple of bedrooms that were bare of comfort, she found one with flowered and silk-lined drapes at the window. As soon as she switched on the radiator, the atmosphere began to feel cosy. On the polished floor there was a shaggy pink rug and she dragged it to lay beside the bed, which she made up with crisp new sheets and a puffy quilt, all fresh and sweet-scented from the shelves in a spacious airing cupboard, which was located in an alcove, near bedrooms on the top floor of the mansion.

A chest of drawers, painted white, stood beneath a mirror and the folding bed, carried into the room by Ian and neatly placed in a corner, was soon ready again, for Peter.

* * *

On the morning following the arrival of their waifs from the storm, Maria was making coffee for herself in the kitchen when Boy and Jaff launched themselves into a scuffle in the wide hallway, displacing mats and knocking a pile of books from a polished circular table which stood beneath the telephone attached to a wall. Maria heard them growling and thudding about, and she also heard the crash when the books fell down.

She set her cup on its saucer, called the dogs and sent them into the garden through the French windows which led onto lawns behind the long sitting room. Then she returned to tidy up the mess they left behind them. Stooping, she straightened a couple of mats before collecting together the fallen books. She considered returning them to the library but she had already noticed that Robert had a habit of leaving books around the mansion and often they were lying open, or were marked with a slip of paper between the pages. It would be sensible to make quite sure he agreed to them being tidied away.

When the telephone rang, Maria hesitated for a moment, then picked up the receiver. At first, Mrs Moss was reluctant to leave a message but when Maria explained that Robert and Ian had shut themselves into one of the studies with instructions not to disturb them, that lady declared the household (which consisted now of Robert, Ian, Maria, Amelia and Peter) was becoming too much for her and she would not return.

Mrs Moss usually arrived to begin work at midday. She washed and tidied away breakfast things; then she prepared a light lunch for Robert and Ian. She took care of the cleaning duties which were hers in the kitchen, and also made checks of the studies and the library, to pick up empty coffee cups when they had been left there. During the afternoon she always cooked the evening meal, staying to serve it before she returned to her own home later. She had a multitude of other responsibilities, including keeping indoor plants watered and the numerous vases of flowers looking fresh.

When Amelia entered the kitchen, Maria told her about the call and together they wondered how many difficulties would ensue. Robert and Ian were still shut inside their study, so the two young women had time to decide how to help. Considering Maria's employment, it was obvious that she wouldn't take on the preparation of every meal but Amelia was eager to help in that regard. "It gives me a chance to say *thank you!*"

Surely, it would be quite a task to cover all the housekeeping duties; yet Maria and Amelia thought they would manage very well between them. They would care for themselves, as well as the men and the little boy. In fact, new visitors arrived just as they tackled chores in the kitchen and things suddenly started to work out very well.

* * *

Amelia began to enjoy finding her place in the house. Refreshed after her night's sleep and supplied with coffee, she relaxed, chatting and helping Maria, who, after the horses were settled for the early part of the day. turned her attention to some of the work normally whisked though by Mrs Moss. For Robert's lunch and perhaps for Ian if he made himself present, they shared the preparation of a quiche and made a fresh fruit salad.

Amelia and Peter were shown the library, where they found another selection of children's books to add to the ones Maria put in their room. Peter happily spread them over a table top. The dog, Jaff, had taken a liking to him and rested his massive head on the child's knees.

There came the sound of a car's engine and tyres on stony ground; looking through the window the women could see a sleek silver vehicle drawing up near the front of the house. Maria wiped her hands on a towel and went to tell Robert he had visitors!

At the front door, there stood a man and a woman, dressed in greatcoats, fur trimmed hats and leather boots. They were surrounded by many cases and bags full of belongings, and they were beaming and pleased to see Robert. It was clear they had come to stay!

Robert rose gallantly to the occasion. Smiling, he extended his hands to grasp theirs. With every appearance of delight, he greeted them warmly. "Welcome brother! My dearest Margaret! Come in!"

He helped the pretty, middle-aged lady to remove her coat, then gave her a hug and a kiss on the cheek. "It's lovely to see you! Come into the lounge, and warm yourselves," he invited them. "We will take your bags up in a little while. What would you like to drink?"

Nigel asked for a whisky and water. Before he shed his heavy outer garments, he returned to the car and collected a beautiful hamper, with leather straps buckled around it. Opened carefully by Margaret it proved a handsome gift. Beneath crackling cellophane were preserves in glass jars, liqueur chocolates, luxurious iced mince pies, tinned shortbread, a beautiful Christmas cake and bottles of champagne. While Nigel settled himself in the easy chair opposite Robert's own, the old man went to mix drinks at his cabinet; meanwhile, Margaret declared that she longed for a cup of tea. She went into the kitchen to make it herself. She was obviously familiar with her surroundings.

Maria could tell there must have been some confusion, especially when Robert looked up from his drinks tray and gave her a meaningful wink! She quietly made a dash for the stairs, went to the next floor and found an attractive double room. The air inside was very cool but she switched on a radiator and swiftly made the bed, with fresh sheets and blankets as well as a thick quilt.

"This is becoming a habit!" Maria thought. However, she had quite enjoyed preparing Amelia's room and was happy to turn her attention, now, to a creating a suitable welcome for Robert's new guests. There would be plenty of time for the heater to warm the air before the couple needed to go to bed, she thought. She had spotted folded dusters on a shelf inside the airing cupboard, alongside neat piles of clean sheets. She collected two, made one slightly damp, and whisked a thin layer of dust from the surfaces and the mirror of a dressing table, then energetically polished the glass to a shine with the other.

She peered into the en-suite bathroom, which was spotless and well supplied with folded towels. It had an array of room fragrances, in glass bottles rowed up on the window sill. Maria hung a fluffy white hand towel on a silver ring beside the sink and selected a freesia scent to squirt into the air. There were spare rolls of toilet tissue, fresh face flannels and new bars of soap in a cupboard. She found and opened a box full of soft cosmetic tissues in pastel colours, to place on the bedside table. A cosmetic mirror lay on a folding stand on the sill above the sink and she set it up, propped for use.

There was a trio of rosebud patterned porcelain dishes on a window sill; Maria wiped those too and arranged them before the swing mirror on the dressing table, for Margaret's jewellery and lipsticks. Another generous spray of scent and the suite really seemed freshly cared-for. Then, reminding herself she was in a hurry, she decided the suite was ready for Robert's guests. It would be nice for Margaret, if she decided to come up to her room for a rest, to find the preparations all complete! Maria made her way back along the landing and down the wide staircase.

* * *

Amelia had left her cottage so fast; she hadn't been able to pack many belongings. She had just a few items; her handbag slung over one shoulder, some clothes in a carrier bag and others which had been scrambled into her arms in seconds. Before long, Maria and Margaret hunted through their own possessions to offer her sweaters and soft trousers. She was tiny but Maria was slim too, so they rolled up the trouser legs and the sleeves of a couple of cardigans. Margaret's woollens were more capacious but they were warm and fragrant with fabric softener. They made Amelia look elfin and rather sweet.

Peter was a patient child and did not seem to suffer from shyness. He enjoyed a warm bubble bath after breakfast on the first day of his stay, then tolerated being dressed in clothes, old but clean, found in trunks in Ian's room. Left over from Ian's teenage years, they were too large for the little boy but with a good deal of folding and careful belting around his middle, somehow the women made an outfit he could wear. For her part, Amelia was very grateful to be there in the welcoming atmosphere, but there was no doubt she struggled at first, feeling shy. Before long, Margaret proposed making cakes, which meant the three women shared the familiar task in the warmth and chaos of the kitchen, drinking tea, bumping into one another and, eventually, laughing together.

As the cakes baked, filling the room with a delicious scent, Maria went to stand near the fire in the sitting-room, which was empty except for the two dogs sleeping on their blankets. The men were playing a game of snooker in the library. She untied her plait, having found cake crumbs in it and separated the long strands with her fingers. She noticed the younger woman had entered the room and was watching her, looking faintly wistful.

"Amelia, pull *your* hair down! I think it would look really pretty! Why do you tie it up so tightly?"

Amelia said she didn't know. She always wore the same style.

They went upstairs to Maria's room, where Amelia sat at the dressing table and they took pins and the elastic band from the tightly twisted fair knot. Released, the cascade of fine hair was silken and curly. Maria carefully ran a comb through it and, with Amelia's agreement, used a pair of scissors from the drawer in the kitchen, to trim a few layers until shorter fronds curled and clung around the young woman's heart-shaped face.

"It is too curly!" Amelia observed, without too much concern. She leaned forward in her chair, frowning at her changed reflection.

"No, I don't think so, Amelia!" Maria separated and twirled ringlets around her forefinger, making more curls. "Your eyelashes are curly too! I think you look just right!"

* * *

At the age of sixty-eight Nigel was Robert's younger brother. Like Robert, he was very courteous and didn't assume an obvious air of superiority over any of his companions. He liked taking on his share of the household chores, always deferred to his wife and was easy company for everyone.

Florid in complexion, twelve or more years younger than Robert, Nigel was energetic, loud and occasionally voluble but there was no harm in him at all. Boy and Jaff adored him and lay by his feet when, obedient to his wife's instructions, he sat at the kitchen table to peel vegetables for dinner.

"I don't very warm …" he complained when he felt chilly, pulling a massive sweater over his head.

"Is he one for saying odd things?" Maria wondered. "Or does he say ordinary things oddly?"

He recounted endless stories, each with only the vaguest conclusion, putting the knife down on the tablecloth as he gesticulated until Margaret scolded him and finished the peeling herself. Sometimes Nigel's tales were fascinating and Maria was entertained by them. She would sit opposite him, scraping potatoes or stirring mixtures which Margaret placed in bowls before her.

"When I was a boy," Nigel would begin, and follow this with a tale of a tame jackdaw that could mimic human voices, or stories about spending long summer days in the countryside with friends who plundered neighbours' orchards, or adventures when he went swimming in ice-cold rivers where the boys made muddy slides down banks to make their splash landings into the water all the more exciting. (Could jackdaws mimic humans? His listeners weren't sure!)

There was an answer to Maria's mild interest in Ian's activities, when conversation between Nigel and Margaret revealed that he was possessed of plenty of old money (as they termed the family inheritance) and could choose how to spend his days. Nigel confessed that he had plenty of respect for Ian, who was a hard worker. Since his grandfather owned many acres of surrounding land, Ian managed the farms that were scattered upon it, some of them at quite a distance from the mansion.

A Dispute

The day that followed the arrival of Margaret and Nigel was cold but heavy rain had stopped falling. During the evening, Ian had said he would not ride that day, so Maria rode Cass and led the other horse. They were both fun to ride but since Ed stood a few inches shorter than Cass, it made sense to lead him.

The ride was muddy and, on her return, Maria had a good deal of work to do, cleaning the horses' legs and hooves. The harness was spattered with dirty water from puddles in the fields and it was some time before her careful work made it shine again.

By ten o'clock, Ed and Cass were groomed, fed and settled in clean stalls. In Maria's cubby hole of a tack room, brasses gleamed and leather was supple and glossy. She had developed a routine she loved and was inclined to feel proprietorial about the tidy stables and the comfort of her charges.

Maria began to walk away from the stables, feeling ready to make some coffee and take a break. She was startled when Ian strode past her, with a shout. "Riding!"

Maria paused in her walk across the yard. "I've exercised them both, already!"

He waved in acknowledgement but he disappeared into the tack room, then emerged bearing a clean saddle and bridle. He turned, and entered the stables. Worried, Maria found she couldn't leave the stable yard. She hesitated, then found a broom and pointlessly swept while she waited. Ian and his actions were not really her business but she hoped he would see the horses eating and leave them in peace. Instead, after a few moments he reappeared. Foolishly already mounted, he had to duck his head as he rode through the doorway of the stable block; then he turned Cass and made for the fields.

Maria stood watching, the broom in her hand. Inside, she was incandescent but there was no time to remonstrate. In moments, he was off, urging Cass to break into a trot, swiftly followed by a canter. At a field entrance made muddy by tractor wheels they paused for a second, then sprang forward into a gallop. Maria could see them for a moment longer as they sped along a track on the edge of woodland, but they were soon out of sight.

She went over to the house and into the porch to change her riding boots and could hear the two dogs pawing at the other side of the door. They were in the passage which led to the kitchen and then the great hallway. Undecided, she stood there in stockinged feet for some moments, then her sense of duty made her release them to join her. She pulled on a pair of wellington boots and took the dogs out-of-doors for a few minutes, but then she returned them to the house, thinking Robert might look for them before her return. She could not go on calmly with her normal routine; she had made up her mind to take some time for herself. Pulling a scarf from her pocket to wrap around her neck, Maria left, walking quickly, trying to deal with her anger.

She walked, squelching in her boots through muddy patches on the pathway, going on until the first flood of adrenalin was over and some hopeful thoughts came into her mind along with a calmer feeling. Animals need good care; they thrive on routine and inevitably it was hard for Maria to let that routine go. She was conscientious about her duties and yet, going over events, she knew that, exasperating though Ian was, he would do the horse no real harm. She was aware of a slightly obsessional tendency within her; she liked to work according to the same plan each day.

Cass was a placid horse and he was healthy. He would doze later, forget the startling extra gallop and bear Ian no grudge! As an employee, it wasn't Maria's place to argue with Ian in any case. Her thoughts began to make sense and the initial intense annoyance eased. Tiring, she sat down on a stone wall. She watched, only half-attentive, as a man dressed in a long coat with the collar turned up against the cold wind and a tweed cap pulled low over his forehead, followed a small flock of sheep up the hillside. It was not good weather for sitting still and Maria raised a hand to draw her fur-lined hood forward to cover her head and brow.

Two border collie dogs guided the sheep, but they kept circling back. Lagging behind, an ewe was considerably hampered; hopping awkwardly, it had one foot caught in a tangled length of orange twine. Maria stood and made her way towards the farmer, coming up to him from his left. He turned and looked at her, with dark eyes above the thick scarf that bound the lower half of his face. The wind was so brisk it caught her breath, so she simply pointed at the ewe. The dogs were sent to separate the ewe from the flock and, while the other sheep huddled dimly together for a few moments, the man grabbed the struggling animal and expertly tipped her onto her hindquarters. Maria went to help, thinking to disentangle the twine.

"Careful! She'll kick hard!" He felt in his pockets and withdrew a small knife, then quickly cut the rope and pulled its strands away. Maria grasped the jerking leg, hanging on as best she could. During this exercise, the two dogs flattened themselves on the ground, eyeing the flock. In seconds the ewe was released and trotted away unharmed, to join her mates.

"Tea?" The farmer pointed towards a small cottage set amongst outbuildings at some distance away. Maria nodded, clutching at her collar, aware that she was quite cold. They went on, unable to converse properly as the strong wind whipped around them, snatching away their words. He glanced at Maria. "You're well used to animals, I think!"

She nodded and forced a few words from her lips. "I'm a groom."

"Ah!" He accepted her brief explanation. She was capable around working animals. "A groom? It's a great job."

In a yard beside the small dwelling, a dozen brown hens emerged from a hut when they heard the sheep bleating and sensed activity but they crouched, with feathers ruffled when gusts of wind hit them. The dogs did their work without instruction and the herd was penned, quickly and safely inside a barn with great double doors. A single stable was empty of an occupant, it seemed. Noticing Maria's glance, the farmer pointed towards a paddock nearby where a bay cob grazed, well rugged-up. He collected a bucketful of corn from a container before he locked the barn and, when he emptied it into feeders inside the hut, the hens soon hurried back up their ramp.

Inside the tiny house, the farmer unwound his scarf and she saw he was very heavily bearded. She thought it was hard to guess his age, mainly because of the beard but also because he had a weather-beaten appearance. He wore a solemn expression and there were frown lines between his dark eyebrows. Perhaps he was younger than he looked? He indicated a chair by the hearth with a gesture and a nod, then crossed the room to a stove, where he boiled water in a small pan placed on the hob and prepared to make tea.

"He's a man of few words!" Maria thought. Before sitting down, she went, faintly shy, to the sink, where she washed debris from the sheep's fleece from her hands, soaking her fingers with water which ran only cold, turning a cracked bar of orange soap over and over to try to make suds and get rid of the oily feeling. She found a clean towel nearby.

The tea was made by then, and a steaming mug was handed to

Maria. She clasped it gratefully with her cold hands that smelled, now, of coal tar. A large, white cat was curled like a cushion at the back of a deep fireside chair. Maria perched on the chair, in the available space. Soon, she transferred the mug to a low table and pushed her hood back, freeing the long plait of silken light-brown hair and drawing it, with a habitual gesture, over her shoulder.

The farmer's hair was flattened by his cap which he removed to hang up with his heavy coat, on a hook near the door. "I'm Elis," he said. She was gently shifting the cat to make more room for herself. "That lazy thing in your chair is called Smoke."

"Smoke?" She ran gentle fingertips over immaculate white fur. The cat stretched and purred, then tucked a pink nose beneath its forepaws. "Not Snow? What are the dogs' names?" She leaned forward to rub the rough black-and-white coats of the pair, where they lay before a crackling fire. Warming up, they panted a little and their heads were raised as they watched their master with bright eyes. They thumped shaggy tails on the ground upon hearing their names. "Seb' and Jess," Elis said. He went on. "I found the cat. He was so dirty, I thought he was grey!"

"A rescued cat? Poor fellow!" She stroked the cat's head. "You're lucky now, aren't you?" Smoke purred harder, decided her lap was a better option than his corner and crept onto her knees.

Maria felt glad of the blaze in the hearth. She slid her arms out of her jacket and let it fall near her feet as she sipped her tea. Relaxing with the familiar presence of animals around her, she sensed Elis' uncertainty and decided to offer an explanation of her presence on the hillside. "I'm here to work at the Manse for a month. I came to look after the horses and dogs!"

"Ah … yes …" He bent to load the fire with extra wood and was quiet for a few minutes, placing strips of kindling over the hot coals that were sinking into embers, then adding a log or two until flames began to leap again. Each small task made his frown deepen then recede and even when he turned and regarded Maria there was a sober expression in his dark eyes. "I hope Robert gave you a good room?"

"It's *lovely!*" Maria confirmed. "It's far more luxurious than I expected!" Staring into the leaping flames she was unaware that the farmer, sitting back in a chair facing hers, gave her another careful glance.

Before long, with her drink finished and her fingers and toes nicely warmed, she thought it time to leave. She stood, carefully sliding the cat back into his place before taking her empty mug to the sink. She stooped to pick up her coat.

They had spoken only of ordinary things but the hour was pleasant. Elis said he expected that she would enjoy the month ahead. Since she would be riding out, perhaps he would see her again. He hoped she would not get chilblains. At that, she smiled and looked for an answering grin but the slim, weather-beaten face beneath the covering beard was solemn still.

* * *

Maria trudged downhill. Light, icy rain veiled the countryside around her but the route was straightforward; she had pointed herself in the right direction for the parklands. She thrust her hands into the pockets of her hacking jacket. She had been wearing her riding gear throughout the morning and now, out-of-doors again, she felt damp and chilly. Her cheeks were frozen. She began to look forward to the comfort of her own room, and planned to have a hot shower and a change of clothes.

Too numbed by the cold air to feel uplifted, nonetheless she knew she had enjoyed her visit with Elis. His croft was obviously a man's home but it was spotlessly clean, the fire was bright and warm, the animals well-tended and content. Maria liked the fact that Elis had rescued the stray cat.

Her thoughts returned to Ian and his casual treatment of the horse. She had a responsibility to ensure the animals were safe and well. This was her job and the reason for her arrival at the Manse in the first place. Also, it was her passion. Embarrassing though the confrontation might be, she resolved to set aside awareness that it was not really her place to argue. She would tell the headstrong young man how she felt!

In the event, it was not difficult.

Leaving her boots in the porch, Maria went upstairs straight away and headed for her room and her shower. Refreshed, she put on a comfortable denim skirt and a long dark-emerald woollen sweater, which seemed to lend a hint of deep green to her sea-coloured eyes. Finally, she pulled on a pair of black tights, slipped her feet into soft indoor shoes, then brushed her hair and twisted it into a short plait, leaving some of it in a ponytail that fanned out across her back, affected by static electricity.

Feeling better, she made her way down the wide staircase and Margaret peered from the kitchen doorway, calling out with an invitation to share lunch at the kitchen table. "I'm making toast and bacon! Come, before Ian eats everything!"

The aroma of fried bacon was irresistible and Maria was ready to eat after a long morning and the trek back from Elis' cottage. She walked into the room which was cosy and welcoming but the burden of what she needed to say was on her mind and she hesitated after stepping through the doorway.

"Ian …"

He was leaning with his back against a worktop. He seemed to know what was coming, and forestalled her words.

"Maria, I'll check with you before I take the horse out next time! I'm sorry, if you were cross!"

She felt a little overwhelmed by such a ready apology and gladly bent to greet Jaff and Boy, as they came with wagging tails to her side. After a moment, she looked up and regarded Ian in a considering way.

"Heh," he smiled. "I know you already, Maria! I saw your face! I thought about it. Look, don't worry. I made Cass comfortable. I rubbed him down and put his rug back on. He was eating again, when I left him."

Margaret was piling thick slices of toast and hot, crispy bacon into a shallow ovenproof dish, which she had heated. She held it carefully in a gloved hand and placed it on a folded tea towel, with forks handy. She shook her head over Ian's words but made no comment.

Maria sighed. "Alright." She hadn't anything much to say, after all. She suspected Ian knew exactly how to appease people but she was ready to let her annoyance go.

Ian courteously handed her a plate and she accepted it, buttered toast for herself and stabbed some bacon with a fork. She made a sandwich and held it in both hands, feeling relieved.

Maria had enjoyed her walk and the visit with Elis. She liked the comfort of the hearth and the peaceful atmosphere, with the cat purring while the tired sheepdogs rested. Was Elis too serious to be great company? Compared to Ian and his cheerful but somewhat forceful nonsense, she privately decided she rather liked the farmer. There was quite a contrast, too between the humble cottage and the great mansion. Minimal comfort was there in the croft but perhaps it was enough? She had been welcomed, offered a warm place to sit, shared good-natured conversation and was supplied with tea. She had enjoyed meeting the friendly animals. Much the same as things here, decided Maria ... minus all the luxury!

She was quiet, aware that the activities of her day so far had tired her but she did not feel uncomfortable near Ian now and her irritation had genuinely eased with the information that the horse was happy. Margaret poured tea into a white-and-yellow mug and joined Maria at the table. She reached out and gave Maria's ponytail a motherly stroke with her free hand, then withdrew it hastily. "It's got static in it! Ow! It's pretty, though … like the colour of warm honey!"

"Or nuts?" Ian rudely suggested. Maria gave him a horrible frown but if she meant to stop him teasing her, she was unsuccessful. He lost a faintly subdued air. "You've forgiven me!" Preparing to leave the kitchen, he shamelessly handed crusts and bacon rinds to the dogs before rinsing his plate under a tap. "You're lovely, Maria."

"No!" She couldn't be bothered to be cross. She saw Margaret glance at her face and they exchanged a faint smile.

"A *wonder*, then?"

"If you must." Maria had finished eating. She permitted herself an obvious yawn, although in deference to Margaret's presence she held up her palm. She would not meet his eyes, knowing such defiance could easily become flirtatious.

Ian left the two women at last and Margaret made a comment. "You handle him well! Also, you do it in a way that's more than he deserves, really! He is so sure he can charm everyone and he does like to be in control. It's not altogether his own fault. His parents have indulged him and they are very proud of him."

She was going to add something, saying "mind you, *both* …" but Maria, whose thoughts were occupied with Elis again, began to speak simultaneously. They laughed and Margaret didn't go on. Instead, Maria began to describe her walk and Margaret abandoned her half-finished sentence.

"I met a farmer when I was up on the hillside!"

Margaret's attention was caught. "Which farmer?" she wondered. "There are a few about!"

"Someone with a really heavy beard," Maria said, dismissively, wanting to talk about Elis' animals more than she cared about describing him! "I wasn't sure how old … sort of, fortyish, maybe … or younger …"

"Ah," Margaret smiled. "More tea, Maria?" She got to her feet and poured fresh tea for both herself and Maria, then returned to the table and prepared to listen. Hearing about the animals, the croft and the courteous but dour farmer, Margaret was sure she knew who the man was. "Well, as it seems you know, since you both got acquainted, that's Elis. He isn't old; he's only in his thirties. We have to respect him; he likes his privacy. I think he even enjoys solitude as a rule, up there at Shepherd's Lot! Were you really invited to stay for tea?"

Maria described the plight of the ewe.

Margaret could imagine the scene. "Yes, he *would* like a woman who is good with livestock. If you hadn't been interested and helpful, I doubt you'd have been invited inside! He sets great store by the animals. He's very careful with them."

Maria was about to leave the room, but first she went across to the sink to wash her hands. She twisted the taps and hot water came out of the taps with a force, hitting the empty bowl noisily so that Margaret's next words were almost lost. "They all are."

* * *

When Maria awoke the following day, her mind was full of thoughts which she must have been processing in her sleep. Her dreams had been confused, with visions of chilly hillsides, horses and sheep but, once she began her morning routine, she found herself reviewing some of her experiences since she arrived to begin her job.

Showered and clothed, she made a hot drink on the little table in her room, where there was a minute kettle, one clean white mug, teaspoons and all the sachets of coffee, tea, long-life milk and sugar she needed. Then, she wandered from her bedroom, across the polished floor, to the opposite side of the long upstairs corridor, where she stood on a faded rug with her cup of coffee clasped in both hands to look through a narrow window at the parkland. It was a peaceful scene and there was a frosty appearance to the grassy spaces, where a few wild creatures were visible. Rooks were feeding. A hare appeared near the boundary of the gardens, then vanished beneath a hedge.

There were blue hyacinths in a saucer on a windowsill. The warmth of a radiator sent their sweet, powerful fragrance into the air, and seemed to enhance her enjoyment of the beauty of the scene, the comfort in her surroundings, and a sudden surge of happiness in her heart.

Maria's expectation was only to care for horses and dogs. She hadn't given much thought to Robert, who would surely be a rarely seen figure. In advance of her arrival, she didn't know his grandson shared the house. When the job arrangements were made, it seemed her lodgings during the weeks of her employment would be the groom's flat above the stables. There were no plans for a young woman and a little boy to join the house guests, and if Maria might have imagined visitors would share the Christmas period, she never expected to spend time with them all.

Maria's own family were not without privilege. Her father was a well-respected academic, and her mother had inherited property from her parents. Maria and her brother and sister had always been well cared for, enjoying a comfortable life in their sprawling, detached bungalow in Suffolk, where lawns, an apple orchard and extra land surrounding the building and as a child Maria had been able to own her own pony. Nevertheless, coming to the Manse on a work footing, she hadn't anticipated finding herself virtually a house guest and a part of everything.

Heavy footsteps could be heard, a friendly *hello* interrupted her musings and Ian strode along the hall behind Maria. She pulled her thoughts back to the moment and turned to say an answering *good morning* to his retreating back.

Margaret

Margaret, a lady in her late fifties, was Nigel's second wife and it was obvious he thought himself lucky to be married to her. Who would have guessed, he beamed, very happy to discuss the subject, that he would find *another* beautiful person, after his first dear wife passed away, to love and care for? He admired her. There was no doubt that, in her turn, she loved him too.

Margaret took a keen interest in eating healthily but she struggled to keep her weight in check. She enjoyed making vegetable dishes and knew the value of simply steaming fresh carrots or broccoli or other greens to serve them with a shake of black pepper or herbs, but she favoured a drizzle of melted butter. She also knew how to make wonderful rich cheese sauce for cauliflower, or creamy white salt and pepper sauce for pasta. A roast dinner simply had to be accompanied by a Yorkshire pudding, and freshly made pizza was best served with garlic bread … so the generous bowls of salad which she placed on the dinner table were inevitably boosted considerably by many more calories! What with tasting dishes before she served them, and her healthy enjoyment of a wide range of food, it was a losing battle for Margaret to try to keep slim.

She favoured a typical outfit composed of a wool skirt and a blouse topped with a neat cardigan, which sported pearl buttons or a sparkling brooch. Her clothes were often in bright shades such as raspberry pink, sulphur blue or emerald green. She kept her hair in neat, short layers, dyed light blonde and lacquered well.

Maria found herself comparing Margaret with her friend, Sheila, who also fought a tendency to gain weight. However, Margaret had no need to dress in drab outfits. She wasn't affected by the unwelcome interest of someone like Phyllis, with her dreadful envy. Nigel bought jewellery for his beloved wife and encouraged her to wear attractive clothes in feminine colours.

Surely, she could hardly have had any former life other than that of a nurse, for she was very bossy! However, no-one minded. As the days went on and Amelia and Maria made her acquaintance, they saw that she was truly and fundamentally very kind indeed, with none of the abrasive impatience affected by some nurses as a result of the power they often inevitably have over patients.

* * *

Soon after her arrival at the Manse, upon learning that the redoubtable Mrs Moss had left poor Robert *in the lurch* (as she termed it) Margaret announced her intention to keep house and she would not be deterred.

"It's a very good thing that Nigel and I are here earlier in December, compared with other Christmas times," she told Maria and Amelia, unwittingly clearing up a lingering sense of confusion in Maria's mind. The couple had obviously arrived before their rooms were ready!

"Maria has the horses and dogs to see to," Margaret reasoned. "Amelia must watch Peter and besides she is not used to the place. Ian …"

She left a meaningful pause, but the women realised that, in any case, she was happy to find herself with a useful role amongst their group!

"Besides …" she explained with an air of settling the matter as she tied herself contentedly into an apron and began to assemble cooking pots. "Nigel is going to help me!"

No-one could argue! She appointed herself their cook-house-keeper, and that was that.

PETER

At six years of age, dark-haired Peter was very self-possessed. He had such a ready understanding and was so keen to carry out instructions correctly, it did not go unnoticed by the occupants of the old house.

"How does he get on in school?" Maria wanted to know. "Surely, he's way ahead of his age group?"

Amelia confirmed the child had been identified as being very able and although this made her proud, she had concerns for him. "Nothing is easy, is it? He may have great chances ahead because of his high intelligence, but at the same time, I would hate it if he got bullied."

When she took a cup of warm milk for Peter, who was kneeling on the rug near Robert's armchair, he acknowledged her. "Thank you, Amelia!" The words were said with perfect enunciation and a dignified air to rival Robert's. He was carefully tidying his felt-tipped pens, grouping them according to colour.

"Mum, to you!" Amelia told him.

* * *

Peter could not be found one afternoon and everyone hunted through the house. They felt sure the child must be safe, possibly hiding within one of the rooms, but he didn't respond to calls and poor Amelia became upset. "I'm sure he's okay," she agreed when

Margaret tried to comfort her. "It's just that I can't see him!"

At last, an exclamation from Ian alerted them all: he had found the child. Peter had crept behind the floor-length drapes in the sitting room and he was curled up, fast asleep, on the carpet. Amelia was so relieved, she lost her strength quite suddenly, sat down in Jaff's basket and began to cry.

Peter was brought to her in Ian's arms and deposited into her lap where she still sat in the dog's bed. He nestled into his mother's embrace. "What's wrong, Amelia?" he asked her.

A Playful Episode

"I heard you on the treadmill," Maria was stuffing hay into nets for the horses, when Ian entered the stables one morning. "I should think you might just as well jog a few times around the school!"

"Getting freezing cold?" Ian countered. "No way!"

He had a saddle over his arm and a bridle on his shoulder because he had ridden Cass for an hour. During the previous evening, he told Maria he would ride that day. They had been getting along well since they both made sure to communicate with one another. When Ian let her know his intentions to ride, she would exercise Ed and leave the other horse groomed and ready for him to collect when he was ready. It was reasonable, in that it felt like a normal part of her job.

"Well now, how does that make sense?" Maria wondered aloud. "Here you are, getting freezing now!" She shook her head, as if to underline the mockery in her words.

Ian said he felt better if he jogged in the warm, and anyway, riding out didn't make him feel cold. The argument was getting confusing. Maria was just thinking that she, herself, rather enjoyed an early swim in a heated pool just ahead of a ride! She might have said so, to find agreement and common ground, but Ian wanted to keep the argument going.

"So, you might as well be a bit nicer to a lad who just wants to keep fit!"

He was challenging her. Maria was conscious that she was probably unwise to tease him in the first place but his words made her grin. He was hardly still a *lad!* He was tall and strong, and at thirty-four years of age (according to Robert) he was the same age as herself. She stood straight, facing him and laughing. He rounded on her, picked her up in his arms and threw her into masses of straw where it had been piled against the wall of the stable. Maria stopped laughing and scrambled out of the broken bales wearing a fearsome expression.

Ian saw it and went to her side. "That's fresh straw! It's clean, just a bit broken up. C'mon, you didn't get dirty!"

Maria didn't care about that. She stamped her foot, crossly. *"What if there had been a pitchfork in there?"* She pulled wisps of straw out of her plait. "You have to assume there may be something dangerous left in loose hay or straw! It's one of the first things I learnt in stables!"

He brushed clinging fragments from her shoulders but he refused to be ashamed. "I absolutely know that you keep things tidier than that!"

Mollified, she smiled but then stepped away from him hastily. She flicked away the last of the wisps of straw, herself. "It's lunchtime!" She wouldn't meet his twinkling eyes.

They walked across the yard, amicable but silent. Ian's hands were in his pockets but Maria's sense that he wanted to reach out to her was acute. She tried to force away her feelings, which were mixed. She was worried in a way, since she had hoped for a straightforward working environment this time. That worry was coupled with a very natural awareness that they had been moments away from a kiss …

Yes, it would have been easy to kiss his laughing mouth. She imagined herself leaning against Ian's chest, being loved and feeling cherished again. Perhaps it was fortunate that Ian wrecked the moment for himself when he gave her a sideways glance. "I know what you're thinking!"

Maria lost her temper again. He was smug! "Oh, my …! *You so don't!*" she retorted angrily.

* * *

A pretty woman can find herself in a tangle of emotions when she aims for nothing more than friendship with a man. A platonic closeness may seem perfectly believable, before (often to her dismay) he reveals, by word or gesture, his longing for intimacy. It may be disappointing with a loss of the easy-going friendship that existed. Any sense of pressure or obligation can lead to guilt. The admiration is, of course, flattering too and that has its effect.

Nevertheless, she would keep her promise to herself, Maria resolved. There was no question of becoming emotionally involved, within this situation. Her relationship with the racing stables manager, when it ended, brought about the end of a cherished position. She had to remove herself from a selfish person, but it was regrettable. After that, the effect she had on the domineering and fearful Phyllis, while it was not of her own making, had created a volatile atmosphere which wrecked her ability to continue working in the same environment.

Maria had learned lessons from her experiences and now she felt determined. She would not risk another episode, with anyone, when the outcome could harm her livelihood. Not even when a potential for a shared fascination was there!

* * *

Maria and Margaret were both early risers, although Maria was often the first to go downstairs in the morning because she was conscious of her animal care duties. When she returned from the stables on the morning after her scuffle with Ian, she found Margaret had set aside the night-time fireguard and was stirring embers which still glowed in the great iron frame inside the hearth. Together, the women added twists of paper, then fresh kindling followed by pieces of wood as flames took hold. The fire provided extra, welcome warmth in the long sitting room and although the whole of the mansion was kept heated by radiators there was clearly a habit and tradition in keeping the fire in.

The fireplace was so vast, they could stand under the brickwork at the front and Margaret, who was not tall, didn't need to stoop. An awful dust was raised when she energetically swept around the fireplace, but she was so engaged in the task, Maria said nothing and went to find a substantial log from the store in a shed near the tack-room. Much burdened by the one she chose, she staggered back towards the doorway.

Ian had seen her from the kitchen window. He was waiting by a couple of shallow steps that led up to the porch. "Give that to me," he ordered, good-naturedly. "It's far too heavy for you!"

Maria was still cross with him since his assertion that he could guess her thoughts. Clutching the log, she insisted she liked to bring in wood, although in truth she knew its weight was too much for her.

"No, you'll hurt your back! I only just spotted you. I would have gone to get another log; at least let me bring it up the steps and indoors!" He took it away from her.

Maria went to sit on a kitchen chair to remove her boots, while he made for the sitting room and the fireplace. After heaving the log into the well-stacked fire, he returned. He observed that Margaret was off upstairs for a shower, saying she was dusty.

"Are you alright now, *Marie*? Do you want coffee?"

This was annoying. A cup of coffee would be nice and yes, she was alright. However, no-one called her Marie! Stubbornly, Maria put her head down.

"You have masses of ash in your hair, too!" he observed.

Maria raised her head at that. She flicked some of the dust and ash from her crown with her fingers. "I'll have to go and wash it out!" She stood up. "It's from the fireplace!"

Perhaps the action reminded Ian of the straw they both removed from her plait and how it happened. He smiled but he kept a respectful distance this time. There was a silence and Maria hesitated. Relenting a little, she said that she would like a cup of coffee. Perhaps he hadn't realised that shortening her name wasn't welcome? He probably meant to be friendly. In any case, he corrected himself. "Okay, *Maria!*"

He reached into high wall cupboards for crockery, set a row of mugs on the counter and began to pour coffee for them both. Maria accepted her drink and carried it with her, heading for the stairs, while Ian, who was about to go into the sitting room, filled an extra cup for Margaret.

This is how we must go on, Maria told herself. *This is friendly but respectful. No more teasing, no more tensions.* She resolved to be very disciplined from then onwards. Tired of analysing every aspect of their confrontations, she would be cooler, from now on!

Riding Out

Riding Ed, Maria found herself turning him away from their parkland routes. She would take him uphill and the extra exercise would be good for his legs. Inevitably, with thoughts of Elis in mind, she remembered his parting comment.

Since she would be riding out, perhaps he would see her again.

How would it seem, if she deliberately rode up to the croft? Was she effectively invited to do so? Not really, Maria knew that! He seemed open to the idea though and after all, did she need an excuse? She decided not to care.

The croft and its surroundings looked peaceful at first. The brown hens were scattered about, freed from their pen, pecking at the hardened ground. Then, the narrow front door of the building opened and Seb' and Jess ran out, barking. Elis followed them. He didn't smile or even greet Maria but he looked up at her as she sat on Ed.

"Come and meet my horse!"

Ben was a cob, not tall, perhaps just making fifteen hands; a height that qualified him as a horse instead of a pony. He raised his shaggy head, watching as they approached.

Maria dismounted from Ed, looped the reins over her elbow, and stood at a respectful distance to look at Ben. He was very stocky and bright bay in colour. His thick dark mane fell into his eyes and cascaded over his neck and withers, and there was feathering on his legs. Maria loved him. He was comfortable inside his single stable. Next to it, there was a lean-to building for tack, hay and straw.

Ben kicked the door and regarded his master with intelligent eyes. "It's because he wants to come out," Elis explained. He put out a hand to take Ed's reins, so that Maria could step closer to the stable.

"He is amazing!" Maria ran her hands over the well-muscled neck and with her fingers she tucked the heavy forelock aside. "A good boy, aren't you?" she told the horse.

"No," Elis shook his head. "He's a handful!"

Ben pushed his muzzle towards her in the friendly way of a well-loved horse but he was a far more capricious animal than either of the hunters owned by Robert. He quickly tired of being stroked and shook his head violently.

Elis was about to go uphill further and check on some pregnant ewes. He handed Ed back to Maria and began to fetch tack from the lean-to. "Ride with me?"

So, together they rode over the rough ground behind the croft, with their faces turned towards a cool breeze. Ed was more lively than usual, flexing his neck and being skittish; he was unused to riding out with Ben. He took silly, short steps and pretended things in the grass scared him.

"Come on, Ed," Maria reproved him. Calmly, she loosened the rein so he could extend his neck.

"That's good," Elis observed. "If you collect him up, he thinks he's about to go off like a rocket!" He had pulled on a battered, brown riding cap. He had his work cut out, with Ben. "This one's always a task, at least for the first ten minutes!" He had to pay attention, so that he was not unseated by the sideways hopping and exaggerated bouncy stride. They cantered, as Ben so obviously needed to use up his energy.

They barely spoke, except to remark on some aspect of their

surroundings. A large bird circled overhead, Elis said it was a red kite.

"Will it go after the lambs, when they come?" Maria wanted to know, but he explained it was more likely to catch smaller mammals such as rabbits and hares. They reined in for a few moments, to watched the bird.

The ewes were grazing on short tufts of grass in the shelter of a pile of giant rocks. Seb' and Jess, running at the horses' heels, were not sent out to round them up. Elis decided they were sufficiently sheltered to remain there, for the time being. He turned his horse around; Maria followed suit, and they began to trot along the sloping ground, heading back towards the croft.

Maria was conscious that Elis was a hardworking man. She didn't want him to think she would waste time, so, as they slowed their mounts to a walking pace, she mentioned her role in Robert's household. "I enjoyed our ride," she told him. "I won't be able to come back all that often …" Did the statement sounded as if she assumed he would want her to keep coming back? Her words tailed off but there was no need to worry; he grasped her meaning.

"No," he agreed. "You've got plenty to do with the hunters and dogs down at the mansion."

Maria hid a smile. She felt an affinity with this quiet man and it was refreshing.

Maria's Story

"Everything is lovely here, isn't it?" Peter was enjoying his days.

In many ways, he was right. He was being kindly treated by everyone around him, and Robert's hospitality was generous. Amelia had offered a confidence during one of their evening chats, and it opened the way for her listeners to understand her early nervousness. Her story was somewhat sad.

"I was isolated, often all by myself when other families are spending time together. My husband said he had to work on weekends. I didn't realise it was odd and when I asked him to stay at home, he would get very angry."

"At last, I stopped questioning him so that I could keep the peace. I tried to fill our days with nice things for Peter … walks, cooking or reading together, visiting friends … but it was hard on a Sunday. Neighbouring families have their own lives; my parents live a long way from here and we were often lonely."

* * *

For Maria, there were occasional surprises.

The assistants in the local shop took an immediate dislike to her and made no effort to hide it. Their names were Sue and Jackie; they were the best of friends, and they dressed in similar outfits, with their hair coloured the same hard shade of reddish-brown.

She approached them with her usual straightforward and pleasant manner but a sequence of events unfolded over the visits.

A big box of crackers for cheese turned out to be soft. "One of us must take them back!" Margaret said. "Those two in the shop mustn't sell us old stuff!"

"I'm sorry," Maria handed the rejected biscuits over to Sue with an apology, as if it were her own fault that they were nasty. Wearing a suspicious expression, Sue replaced them, just about.

Some chocolate-covered buns were stale and somehow, Maria got the job of returning them, too. "They aren't stale," Sue told Maria. "You think they are because they are different from your usual kind!"

Insulted, Maria was moved to point out that, as a newcomer, she had no idea what the usual kind were like. In any case, stale food was old food and not at all the same as a simply *different* flavour!

After that, the ladies served a customer over her shoulder, upon the pretext that they hadn't realised she was ready to be served. They regularly stood in her way so that it was hard to pass behind their backs, as they stacked shelves when she walked around the aisles with her trolley.

Such belligerence would have been the silliest thing ever to get really cross about and Maria tried not to concern herself with it. Since, inevitably, it brought to mind some memories of Phyllis and her unnecessarily controlling behaviour, she made her visits to the shop as brief as possible. She mentioned it to Amelia, who chose to see a funny side to the assistants' antics. "They just don't like you!"

* * *

On dark evenings, by four o'clock in the afternoon lights were switched on in the Manse and soon afterwards the group gathered with drinks in advance of their evening meal.

Maria had an opportunity to talk about her recent work history and found her thoughts were still burdened by memories of the way

Phyllis treated her. Now, she could confide in sympathetic listeners.

"I knew Phyllis was unfair," she said. "I should have ignored her but I got jumpy. I had no warning before she criticised my scarf and my habit of popping a tiny bag over my arm and suddenly, I wondered if I was the one who was strange! It made me keep wondering, *what's next?*"

"No-one wants to be made to feel they are in the wrong when they are doing their best," Margaret said. "Couldn't you have been a bit tougher yourself? Given her a piece of your mind?"

"I felt victimised." Maria remembered those times. "I didn't want a big fuss! My confidence was rocking and I kept weighing things up, feeling unsure of myself. I tried not to show it and as a matter of fact, I felt determined not to involve myself with her invented arguments! There was just one occasion when I weakened, and she was nagging me about timing. My mind was really on my work and, without thinking twice, I did bite back! I told her she shouldn't get onto me for being two minutes late. I even said that was silly!

"Straight away, you would have thought *silly* was a swear word! She was so angry! I had gone and made her much worse."

"Mm," Margaret considered this. "Well, timing matters on a hospital ward and I do remember rushing to make sure I didn't get into trouble. You are right too, because two minutes isn't much and it's pointless to argue over in most cases, especially if your actual boss was unconcerned." She sipped her sherry thoughtfully. "I can't imagine you swearing, Maria!"

"Perhaps I shouldn't have left? It seemed decisive at the time!"

"Don't doubt that," said Robert. "You were all set to get bullied and you got out and saved yourself more of it. I'd say, it's a very good thing you did. You were strong-minded. Anyway, their loss is our gain!"

He became philosophical and held forth about the psychology of controlling behaviour. "Going over the top about a minute or two, when it is not significant can be a sign of a problem personality;

even a flawed one. That person fears being ignored and made to seem less in control. Logically, I am sure you could have made up the fractional loss at midday or coffee-time.

"Not actually your boss, Phyllis nevertheless wanted you to think she could control you, and thought you should fall into line with Sheila, who was unassuming. It's probably no coincidence that Phyllis is physically plain; sometimes you find such excessive response when an individual feels vulnerable for their own personal reasons.

"Clearly, she saw your competence and self-presentation, noticed Sheila liked and respected you, and felt disadvantaged. When she made a fuss about your possessions, implying that you looked impermanent, she had probably guessed that, once you knew how her behaviour could affect you, indeed, you were!

"It's also possible, since you were competent and likeable, she saw you as someone with the potential to impress the boss and thus usurp her position."

"It's complicated!" Amelia tried to follow Robert's logic. "She thought you were different from herself and yet she worried about you stepping into her shoes!" She realised something. "*Phyllis? Phyl* ... it's almost the same as a boy's name!"

"In a way, it all comes from a plain truth!" Margaret, like Amelia, grasped Robert's explanation in part. "It boils down to the fact that Maria's pretty and feminine!"

"If she was a nice person ..." Maria felt moved to clarify some-thing. "I used to think she could stride about and be as mannish as she liked! I had no quarrel with her, certainly not about her ... you know ... ways!"

"No, her choice to appear mannish was her own but still, it's clear your brand of fragile beauty presented her with a challenge. She had feelings of envy, and couldn't handle them." Robert paused. "Not, of course, that you are fragile, Maria!"

"Surely, you did the right thing in getting out?" Margaret

couldn't imagine letting someone like Phyllis be such a bully. "Why let someone who seems hostile have access to you?"

Robert remained in agreement with Margaret. "Before long, trying to please a bully would have wrecked your self-esteem. Don't wrestle with pigs!"

They looked at him in surprise. "*Never wrestle with pigs,*" he quoted. "*You both get dirty and the pig likes it!*"

Amelia chuckled. "Wouldn't that be funny?" She had visualised the scene in a literal way. "No," she went on, "I get it!"

Maria explained how the woman seemed thrilled to be in an argument, pleased when she caused obvious annoyance and satisfied as Maria cleared her desk on the last day.

"She felt like she got rid of you. Well, good luck to her. You wouldn't have been here, if you'd stayed there ..." Amelia stated the obvious. She smiled at Maria.

As they reflected upon their conversation, Margaret realised something and became very honest. "*I'm* quite bossy!"

"Yes," Ian was in the room although he remained silent while the others talked. Now, he joined in. "However, you don't scare us Auntie Margaret! You're not spiteful."

"Neither are you unreasonable!" added Robert, kindly.

"It's because she doesn't need to be jealous," decided Nigel fondly. "She is pretty and clever too!"

"You're a dear!" His wife gave him an affectionate kiss on the cheek, which he accepted as his due.

Maria smiled as Robert nodded in agreement. "That's right, brother; it's a wise summary!" he said.

Ian had listened in silence to the discussion. At last, he had a comment.

"You seem so comfortable around the animals, Maria. It's difficult to picture you in an office!"

"I used to help my father keep his office in order, starting when I was only about sixteen. He's a professor of physics. I liked organising things. For a year after I finished a riding apprenticeship, I went to college and got secretarial skills, and then used them for a few months as a personal assistant to a solicitor. I quite liked it … a bit of admin', talking to people on the phone, meeting clients …!"

Medical Histories

Much pleased by his companions' responses to his contribution, Nigel nevertheless tired of talking. He announced he would go into the study, to read for a while before bedtime. Ian followed him, after topping up his wine glass and collecting a newspaper from the rack that stood near his grandfather's armchair.

Maria felt relieved after discussing her experiences in the office, but the thoughts were stressful while she tried to express herself in a way that her friends would understand, without looking too harsh. The woman, Phyllis, had problems and thankfully those were nothing to do with Maria now. She jumped up, and went into a cloakroom along the hallway to wash her face and hands with cool water.

"We all came here for valid reasons," she mused. "Me, to work. Amelia, unable to get home. Margaret and Nigel, formally invited! Yet, circumstances led us into the situation we're sharing now. I'm glad Abe needed a holiday, just when I really needed to get away from familiar places for a while! We all seem to have so much to talk about!" She dried her hands on a thin, white towel before returning to the sitting room. She had thought of something to ask Margaret.

The group was depleted now that Ian and Nigel had taken themselves off to the study, and the room was peaceful. Maria found a low stool and pulled it over the carpet, to be near Margaret. She said, "I remembered, you said you were glad to be *well enough* to come to visit Robert?"

Margaret nodded. "Yes, I was lucky enough to recover from a rough time." Before she responded further to Maria's query, she continued. "How coincidental that several of us fled something unpleasant. Bullying, unhappiness, poor treatment ..."

Robert agreed. "You are both correct, yet from difficult circumstances people often grow and flourish. After all, we now have a fortuitous situation!"

I do understand what he means, thought Maria. *What an analytical mind he has though!* She turned back to Margaret with a well-meant observation. "I think you are very happily married!"

Maria was impressed by the obviously respectful and loving relationship between Nigel and his wife; she guessed, correctly, that there would be no reason to withhold this comment.

"Yes, I am and thank goodness! I was bullied, last year, *by doctors.* They wanted my fatigue and headaches to be all in my mind, with a mental condition related to my age. They were so judgemental. When I asked to see my medical records, they tried not to let me. So, eventually, although not before I became quite ill, we saw we would have to take the legal route. A solicitor stepped in on my behalf, got hold of my medical files and found there was a lot of silly speculation written as if it was the truth. It was an awful shock.

"Nigel paid for private care and when I finally got a second opinion, it turned out I was deeply anaemic. I needed all sorts of clinical care and medicines!"

Her listeners were aghast.

"Oh, how awful!" Amelia exclaimed. "What happened next? Did you get well quickly?"

"I can't tell you how fast I improved, with the right care! I had suffered and waited for so long. Even as I recovered, I felt traumatised by that ill-treatment. A simple apology from the doctors who let me down would have made such a difference, but no-one was going to offer me that! I don't think they wanted to back down.

"I tried to hide just how harmed I felt. I didn't want poor Nigel to worry over it. I was categorised and dismissed with contempt, and what could he do about it, really? Not at the time, head-to-head with consultants; they think they are so above everyone else. Sorry Robert!" She hesitated. "Present company excepted! You feel so confused because you want to trust them but our best way forward was that second opinion and thankfully, we then met *such* a good, honest doctor." She fell silent, remembering, before finishing her train of thought. "Doctor Pandit. He was so very kind."

The young women turned to Robert, in a natural progression of thought for they knew he was a medical doctor for many years. Ian had explained that he became increasingly dissatisfied with the system, so that when he was in his fifties, he changed and became a counsellor.

"In the medical world," he began, after listening to Margaret's story, "I saw deliberate intimidation, love of power, incipient morbidity where none was indicated and outrageous narcissism."

"So, you changed …" Maria was torn between fascination and fear, considering most people need medical care sometimes.

"Yes. I studied counselling theories and deliberately enhanced my knowledge with the intensive study of psychoanalysis. It is a practice that enables compassion."

* * *

"Bearing in mind that most people do need to see a doctor sometimes, how do we get one we can trust?" Maria spoke with her eyes on the old man's face.

"A good question." He fell silent, sipping iced whisky from a tumbler with a diamond pattern engraved in the glass. They waited and then he went on, pulling no punches. "Many doctors end up being narcissists. They almost cannot help it. Patients look up to them and they are well-protected by the system, even if they make a serious error. If they have no training in psychology or psycho-analysis (and most consider they don't need it) they are not going to spot their own grandiosity ... or, if they are aware of it, the same thing makes them confident of being justified!

"Add a dose of common sense to everything that happens to you. Be aware that doctors see a lot of nasty ailments and you need to be well-informed but that does not mean you must go on a route of being tested for something it is highly unlikely you have! Always have a chaperone and don't accept one of their nurses for that, or they will band together against you in the event that an argument arises.

"If you want a second opinion, remember it's your right. It could also be really sensible to back up your own beliefs, just in case you are missing something important. So, be determined and don't take *no* for an answer if you have become doubtful and if you need bet-ter advice. Research and equip yourself with knowledge if you get diagnosed with something that bothers you. Be open to its truth but be aware it may be a wild theory and, if that issue seems to arise, get a look at your medical records. You have a legal entitle-ment to see them."

He stared into the fire for a few moments, before making an observation. "Patients who trace untruths in their medical diaries will want to change them. While data protection law doesn't permit such a change to the history of a case, it does allow you to add a note of your own, and this must be applied to your file so that you can state and record your point of view."

An expression of sorrow was on his face when he went on. "Never let anyone tell you a loved one must pass in pain. Argue. *Don't leave.* There is medication available. Gain knowledge to sup-port and protect yourself." They were powerful words.

Amelia, like Maria, had seated herself on a low stool, where she faced the fireside with Robert on her right, in his favourite chair.

She had become very serious.

"When I gave birth to Peter," she said, "I was only twenty-one. I was very scared and I knew nothing about pain relief or my rights. The labour started and went on for a few hours at home; then, from the time I was admitted to the maternity ward, it lasted another ten but no-one gave me any medication for the pain! Not even gas and air!"

Margaret was scandalized. "Really? Whatever were the midwives thinking?"

"No." Amelia paused, unconsciously copying Robert's pensive gaze, watching as a green twig sizzled and sparked in the fireplace. "I had practised the breathing exercises really hard, and I have wondered if they thought they would just see if I could do it without help. Like an experiment. No one asked me if I was happy with that, though! I had no pain relief the whole time, although there were midwives around me and they delivered Peter safely."

"But *why?*" Margaret wondered. "It's hard to believe! What was the point of letting you go through it unprotected, like that?"

Amelia had never been provided with an answer to that question. With no experience of giving birth, Maria asked Amelia why she hadn't asked for help.

"I just trusted them at first," she answered. "I thought they knew everything and would guide me. When things got going, I was hot and struggling, so I couldn't really speak or understand objectively what was happening to me. Later, I was just so glad to be handed my baby! He was perfect, after all. I felt lucky."

"That must never happen again!" Margaret said, decisively. "You need someone to look after you!"

Amelia got up from her low seat. "I'm stronger now," she replied. She crossed the room, and was about to go through the open doorway, just as Ian entered the room. They walked straight into one another and recoiled, laughing.

"She does need someone to look after her!" Margaret repeated, while Ian, unaware of what lay behind the comment, smiled down at Amelia.

JUST BECAUSE

On a cold day, Maria hunted for the dogs. She was mystified by their disappearance, since they usually divided their time between following her and resting by Robert's armchair. Although they were fit, they were not young animals and they never showed any tendency to run away.

Margaret had prepared a fire in the sitting room and, once it was burning well, she took in a tray laden with mugs, a sugar bowl and cream jug made of exquisitely decorated, green-and-white bone china. She placed it on a low table beside the easy chair. For the moment, however, Maria's employer was nowhere to be seen.

"He's not in the library or the study, so I think he must be fiddling about upstairs," said Margaret. She collected a steaming, antique silver coffee pot, carrying it carefully before setting it on the tray. She had wrapped a thick, clean tea towel around it. "He'll be down here soon."

Perhaps Boy and Jaff were upstairs too, despite being discouraged from going into the bedrooms as a rule? At last, Maria went back to the stable yard, realising that another logical explanation of the absence of two of her charges was that they had followed Ian when he went out for a ride on Ed. She hoped they had not, since the day was damp and cold. There was even a light frosting of snow on the ground. Trying to control her anxious feelings, Maria reasoned that the pair, both of a working breed, were healthy. Perhaps they would have a thoroughly good run. Nevertheless, she took a broom from its hook behind the door of the tack room and began to sweep, conscious that she did the same thing when feeling anxious before. She made up her mind to be more philosophical, this time!

When Ed trotted into the yard bearing Ian and followed by the dogs, the horse looked hot but alert. The dogs, running behind with tongues lolling, were obviously terribly tired. Maria struggled with her temper for moments before she lost the battle. In a fine mixture of relief and irritation, she let go of her self-restraint and expressed her feelings!

"Why did you do that? Why did you make them run? Boy has sore leg already! How could you?"

Ian dismounted and loosened the girth. "We were going slowly, to begin with. Then, a hare got up," he said, calmly. "They gave chase and I had to wait for them. They are very weary Maria, but they can rest and we'll watch them." He began to lead Ed in circles, walking slowly, letting him cool down.

The dogs gratefully received a newly-filled bucket of water and began to drink. Maria knelt to stroke them. She was genuinely afraid of harm coming to them and they were in her care after all, but she had jumped to a conclusion that wasn't really fair. She felt embarrassed, then worse as her eyes blurred with tears. She had gone too far. She hastily rubbed her eyes with the back of her wrist.

"Maria!" He ran stirrup irons up leathers, loosened the girth, then knotted Ed's reins and looped them over a tethering post. The horse placidly lowered his head and rested one of his hind legs. "Come now!"

She stood up, and he strode over the space between them and took her in his arms before she could turn away, then tightened his embrace when she stiffened, flattening her palms against his chest.

"Take it easy," he said.

He brushed tears away with his thumb, pressed the tip of her nose, gently teasing, smiling into her face. She closed her eyes in an unconscious demonstration of resistance, both against his friendliness and her own vulnerability.

"Just because you have pretty freckles and a honey-coloured ponytail, you are not always right!" Ian told her in his typically shameless way. It was a mixture of insult and kindness.

Maria stopped fighting and stood still, regarding him. "I'm too bossy!"

"No, you are not *too* anything!" Ian answered at once. "Unless it's possible to be too beautiful! I wanted to explain that everything is okay …"

Now, his words were earnest and it was a new development, however his expression was kind and the brown eyes were full of humour. "You worry, don't you? About trust?" She nodded slowly and he let his arms drop to his sides in a welcome sign of respect. Not wanting to be drawn into such a sensitive thread of conversation she returned to their issue. Who was in the right?

"I think of Margaret as the organising one here at the Manse," she confessed. "Not me, I mean. Yet, someone told me once that the things we spot most readily in others are probably character traits of our own. Especially if they rub us up the wrong way!" She hesitated but added quickly, "I love Margaret though!"

"Mm, there's nothing wrong with being looked after by Auntie Marg', she's great!" Ian agreed. "Well now, *Robert!*" To her relief, he become more conversational than flirtatious. "If we are analysing then, *I spot* that you're a determined lady, and I do get that you know what you're doing, with animals!" He was silent for a moment before he declared, "I'm stubborn, too!"

He linked arms with Maria and she recognised the friendly gesture and walked with him. They went into the stable building but there were hay nets to fill and she slipped away from him, feeling that an excuse to drop the close contact was just as well. There was a double meaning in his comment about trust. She was reluctant to let anyone else manage the animals, of course that was true because their care was her job and she was very experienced. Also, she guessed, his comment reflected the fact he would have kissed her, if she had not pushed him away. This was the second time they came so close to sharing a kiss but surely, he could tell, she was not a naturally compliant person.

* * *

Maria hung up nets, while Ian swung opened the door of Ed's stall and swiftly went to collect the horse from the yard. The dogs lay on the flagstones, panting still but not as heavily as before. "We'll take them into the tack room," Maria decided and as soon as the horse was comfortably rugged-up, that was what they did.

She shook out blankets in front of the electric heater and turned it on, and Ian brought in Boy and Jaff, grasping their collars, encouraging them. Their tails were at half-mast but when Maria settled herself with a heap of harness on a bench beside her and cleaning equipment at her feet, they rested, warming their backs near the heater. She began to soak stirrup irons and opened a tin of saddle soap. Ian hunted in the neat cupboards for the stocks of teabags, sugar and dried milk, boiled the kettle and brewed tea. Clasping hot mugs, they shared a companionable silence.

Later, after carefully checking instructions on the packet containing Boy's tablets, Maria doubled his dose, and Ian explained to Robert that the dogs had exhausted themselves. The old man paid a visit to the kitchen to examine his precious animals where they lay near the Aga. Boy opened his mouth in a wide doggy grin and rolled over on his back, and Jaff, who was resting his head on outstretched paws, rolled expressive eyes but looked comfortable.

Robert opened a cupboard beneath the sink and found a bowl that would hold more water than their usual one, spoke to Maria about medication and then took himself off, observing that he thought Boy and Jaff would soon recover.

* * *

Maria felt the need to be alone that evening. She had a word with Margaret to excuse herself from sharing dinner in the dining room, saying she felt tired. In the warm, quiet kitchen, she heated milk for coffee, took a banana from the fruit bowl, filled a crusty roll with ham and salad and with this sustenance stacked on a tray, went quietly upstairs via one of the smaller staircases. At the top there was a narrow door. Maria lifted the old-fashioned latch to open it, then made her way along a dark little passage at the back of the house to access her room.

The comfortable suite was a sanctuary. The sound of the central heating system paused occasionally, then began again with its throbbing note that, weirdly, only seemed to affect the consciousness when it stopped. Maria guessed there was a new frost outside. She put her modest supper on a low unit by the bed, changed into a comfortable pair of grey-and-white pyjamas, and got underneath the covers. Propped against her pillows, she pulled a cardigan over her shoulders and sipped her drink. She reached for a novel, then let it lay unopened on her knees.

Maria was feeling overwhelmed. Suddenly, it seemed she needed to deal with some complicated thoughts and emotions. In removing herself from the family dinner table, and creeping though lesser used parts of the mansion, she was consciously hiding. Her temper seemed sensitive, somehow. Was she becoming unsure of her usual way of coping with the disingenuous Ian ever since she made acquaintance with the dour but attractive farmer? If so, why?

Margaret did not ask questions, but simply nodded acceptance when Maria said she planned an early bedtime, and in any case, this seemed a good idea. After finishing her milky coffee, she found herself slipping into a doze, still pillowed half upright, too weary to care about eating her roll or fruit.

A small sound jerked her awake and she blinked bemusedly at

her alarm clock. About thirty minutes had passed since she lay down in her bed. The room was lit by the glow of a lamp, which she put on when she entered, but corners were in darkness. The sound was a tap at the door, and it came again. Unworried, Maria called, "Come in!" She was pleased to see Margaret's friendly face, with bright blue eyes peeping at her.

"I kept thinking about you! I came to check …" Margaret said, quietly. "Are you okay? Have you got a headache?"

"I'm just tired," Maria said. "I fell asleep straight away. Look, I still haven't eaten my supper!"

"Do you want another hot drink?" Margaret walked over to her bedside and picked up the empty mug.

Maria refused politely. She was grateful for such kind thoughts. She patted the bed beside her legs, stretched beneath the quilt. "Stay?"

Margaret hesitated, then sat down. "I've disturbed you," she said regretfully. "Sorry, Maria!"

"I was only dozing …" Maria decided, all of a sudden, to confide something of the way she felt. Margaret wasn't asking searching questions and this seemed to make it easy to talk about some of her worries. She told Margaret that she lost her temper earlier in the day, and scolded Ian for taking the dogs out. She explained that they were in her care for the time being and, when Ian acted unexpectedly, it bothered her, especially if there could be an unhappy outcome.

Margaret understood. She said, there could be no harm in discussing this with Robert, if Maria wanted to. It was an aspect of her job; she was paid to do it well, and it was up to Robert to deal with Ian if he caused a bother. It was true. Maria remembered Robert's suggestion that she might let him know if any of Ian's words or actions caused her to worry.

She wanted to tell the good-natured woman about the other events. How Ian knew she lacked trust. Certainly, she didn't want him to interfere with the animals, but there was more to the feeling than that. She had difficulties with trusting most men, especially attractive ones. She struggled to cope with Ian's particular brand of humorous interest in her, and at any time she was forced to liaise with him, that interest came to the fore.

She found herself reluctant to say these things. Could she explain them clearly? Margaret had praised her once, and said her way with Ian worked well! Was it fair in any case? After all, she and Ian seemed to have come to an understanding. They had touched on the difficulties as they perceived them, shared tea, cared for the dogs together and got past those awkward moments eventually. Maria didn't want to spoil things now.

Simply, she said, "I will think about that, thank you Margaret! I suspect Ian won't do it again, because we did chat. I don't want to worry Robert. Do you mind if we keep this conversation private?"

Margaret agreed but she looked at Maria's tired face and stretched out a motherly hand to pat her cheek. Margaret was no fool. "Maria, you haven't got to protect Ian. You want to do your job the best way you can. You also have a right to feel comfortable here. I love Ian and I know all his good points. I also know, for sure, that he has some headstrong ways. So, take care of yourself. Remember, I'm here, if you want to talk again."

When the bedroom door closed and Maria was alone, she sighed. Did Margaret think Ian was intimidating her? *Was* he doing that? No, she thought not, after all. She was coping, and all she needed to change was her own tendency to become angry, because the animals here all belonged to the family and everyone was genuinely well-meaning.

Again, Maria experienced a strange sense that her responses to Ian had become somehow affected by her thoughts about Elis. She wondered why this was happening. Time spent with Elis led to serious, straightforward conversation, whereas the best way to cope with Ian seemed to be with laughter.

Was there any need, ever, for her to get sensitive with Ian?

I think he frustrates me! Maria realised. *Partly, because he is truly more irritating than Elis! As soon as I try to be straightforward with Ian, it doesn't work and somehow, I annoy myself!*

She began to settle down more comfortably. All would be well now, she thought. She would make efforts to trust Ian. As for bad treatment, he was not the same type of person as Jason ... She sighed because, yet again, she had strayed into thoughts of the way they saw one another! She had not mentioned to Margaret her sure feeling that she and Ian had almost kissed! Worse, it was the second time they had shared such an intense moment. She wondered how it would seem, if she told Margaret or anyone else, that Ian had once picked her up in his arms? He was being playful but he *was* crossing the line of discretion, considering Maria was in Robert's employment!

* * *

Maria took a sip of water. She put her head on her pillows but sleep wouldn't come and now she felt restless. Sighing, she sat up, thinking perhaps she ought to eat something. Peeling her banana, she found she was still thoughtful; yet, surely, she had come to a good understanding of herself? She felt comforted by Margaret, too. She finished eating the fruit and glanced at the clock again. The hour was not late; just a little after eight o'clock, but the house was quiet. Here, in her room on the top floor, Maria often felt cushioned from the typical sounds of activity. The dogs stayed with Robert during the evenings and their baskets were in the kitchen, where they slept at night. Voices were muted, if they could be heard at all. There was a soft humming sound, made by the central heating system.

Could she fall asleep, if she tried to relax, now?

A second knock came at her door. Was this Margaret again, in nursing mode perhaps, thinking she needed aspirins or tea after all?

"Come in!" Maria called.

She watched the door being opened, heard it brush over the thick pile of the carpet and was astonished to see Ian. He stood still in the doorway. "You weren't at dinner," he said. "I just wondered if … I mean, are you okay?"

"Another one?" Maria thought. Perfectly alright now, she started to grin. So much for her early night! "Come in," she invited him again.

She sat up, suddenly wondering how dishevelled she looked. She put a hand up to her plait of hair and drew it forward over her shoulder.

Ian entered the room, shutting the door carefully. He had no answering grin; in fact, he looked diffident. Maria didn't pat the bed this time. There was a chair placed nearby and he made for it. "Can I …?"

She nodded.

He was freshly showered, with his dark hair in damp curls and the shoulders of his pale grey sweatshirt splashed with water, as if he had pulled his clothes on without fully towelling dry. A faint scent of coal tar soap lingered around him. He was silent for a moment, before asking if there was anything she needed. She ignored this, refusing to offer an excuse for him to visit her room.

Maria felt glad her pyjamas were plain. Most of the lace trim at the neck was hidden by her cardigan. "Ian," she said, in her typically direct way. "Why have you come?"

He hesitated, then tried to explain his actions. "Auntie Marg' said you were having supper in your room. I should have realised … I mean, I didn't know you'd actually gone to bed. I'm sorry, Maria."

All the bedrooms were equipped with tables or desks. Chairs and leather padded stools were tucked beneath them, in case the occupants wanted to eat or work there. The suites were warm and comfortable. His assumption that she was simply eating alone was reasonable, but again Maria consciously made things just a fraction more difficult for him. She answered, "Didn't you see Margaret, just now? She's been sitting with me."

She hoped this didn't make her seem vulnerable. She meant to imply that their talk was private; there was no need for Ian to interest himself.

"No ... uh ... at the dinner table." He hadn't crossed paths with Margaret after she left Maria's room. He leaned forward, resting his elbows on his knees, wanting to get to the point of his visit. "I was wondering ... I mean, I was hoping. Could you, maybe, *start to like me for who I am?*"

It was a fair question on the face of things, but Maria had already struggled with her feelings. In her bed, she felt awkward, without a way to escape the question, acutely conscious of her thoughts of a few minutes before. Still, she recognised an opportunity to clear the air between them and make things better for herself in this lovely place, where she so wanted to stay and see the job through both for Robert's sake and her own. She decided to be as casual as possible, even though it was clear that Ian was not in a carefree mood. On the contrary, he had very nearly lain his feelings bare and he seemed profoundly earnest.

"I do like you, Ian," she answered. "I have to remember that I'm here to work! I was thrilled to be given hunters and dogs to care for and the job is really all I planned to do. I'm determined to do it well."

He was silent. Her glance went to his face, then fell again. She looked down at her hands. She was telling him the truth but it was difficult. There was a feeling for Maria that she was only skimming the surface of her situation now.

"When I arrived here, I thought I would live in the stable block! I love this marvellous house, and the welcome I've been given but I'm so conscious of everything that goes with it ..."

She paused, feeling unsure of a way to express and underline the fact that plunging into a relationship was not her wish. She didn't want to seem rude. Surely, he didn't mind so much that he would feel hurt? A touch weakly, she finished. "Of course, we can share time, especially around the stables. I think, if we just go on a friendly way, we'll be fine."

It wasn't a warm response but it was the best she could do in the circumstances. Maria, herself, had sometimes teased Ian, which must have revealed a certain friendliness at the very least. It crossed her mind to apologise. She decided against it, in case she sounded too personal all over again. She had spoken as honestly as she dared, leaving a few things unsaid and keeping her point of view straightforward.

Ian sat very still and his dark eyes remained fixed on her face while she spoke. She felt a little flush creep into her cheeks but his typically teasing expression was absent. He was listening carefully. If he was thinking about all the fun they'd shared, the laughter and their obvious potential for closeness, he chose not to say so. He didn't call her out for being disingenuous; instead, accepting her words, he blamed himself.

"I keep messing things up," he said ruefully. He straightened in his seat. "I understand what you're saying, Maria." Looking thoughtful, he stood up. "Good night" he said, before making his way across the room and leaving her alone.

HELPING

Peter was out-of-sorts and it was hard to know what might to be done, to cheer him up. Margaret wondered if he was falling ill since his cheeks were flushed, but Amelia confided quietly she thought this was simply because Peter felt cross. He knelt on a cushioned seat and stared out of the window at the bleak, dark night. Freezing sleet beat against the glass. "That rain is mean." He gave a heavy sigh. "All my best things are in my room at home!"

"What are you missing?" Robert asked kindly, looking at the child from his place by the fire.

Amelia went to Peter's side and stroked his fair head. "Let's close the curtains now! Is it your Star Wars men you're wanting?"

No. With a fat tear on his cheek, Peter told them. "Teddy!"

Margaret put her newspapers and spectacles on the arm of her chair, and left the room. Amelia cuddled her son until they saw her return. She was holding a beautiful teddy bear with plush blue fur and a great yellow bow at its neck.

"Nigel gets keepsakes for me, everywhere we go!" she said. "This nice fellow is bored in my room! He would love to live with you, Peter."

The bear was put into the child's arms. He studied its face where the eyes, nose and smiling mouth were embroidered with dark brown cotton. He straightened the golden bow and observed that it was not like Teddy so its name must be different, but he thanked Margaret politely and tucked the new toy into his lap. It was acceptable.

"That *is* a lovely bear," commented Maria. "I would like one like that to sit on my pillow! Are you going to call him Bluey?"

"Yes," Peter agreed at once. "When he gets used to me, you can hold him sometimes!"

"That is very generous, Peter!" Robert peered at the little boy. "Well done!"

"Thank you so much, Margaret!" Amelia had given a little gasp when the bear was presented to her son. Now, she found coloured pens and some paper, and helped him to depict a storm, with giant raindrops falling from grey clouds and splashing into puddles. They filled the page with plenty of dramatic swirls of dark grey. Peter concentrated on the picture, bending over it, colouring in the puddles and clouds until they were very dark. He held his new bear on his lap.

"The storms will be over before long," Amelia told her son. "We will go to find all your things and they will be there waiting for you! You'll see!"

* * *

Maria offered to sweep and dust the library. They were all enjoying the use of the room and access to books, to read when they each settled down to sleep at night. Margaret, Amelia and Maria formed an impromptu book group and shared pieces of the old classics as well as a shorter novel or two, to discuss as they cooked or cleaned the house, or when they sat together in the evenings while Peter occupied himself with his drawings or bricks.

The old gentleman kept a piano there, which was always tuned and ready for use. He could no longer play well, as his hands were becoming arthritic. Sometimes, he would take a soft cloth and some polish to shine up the top. Maria watched him as she dusted and repositioned a row of delicate porcelain vases on the windowsill in the library. She wished she could help him make music but she had never been taught to play an instrument. The view through the window presented a nicer scene today, with the torrential rain having eased and a calm, if sodden, parkland visible.

Behind Maria, the door swung open and Amelia, with Peter beside her, entered the room just then. She went to place a book amongst a set of novels. She turned back. Unexpectedly, she went over to the beautiful piano. "Could I play something?"

"Mum plays the piano at my school!" Peter observed in a matter-of-fact way. "She's got certificates!" He turned his attention to the multitude of children's storybooks, hunting for something new.

Surprised and delighted, Robert immediately consented. Amelia seated herself composedly at the piano. She opened it, and ran her hands expertly over the keys. "What shall I play?"

Eagerly, the old man turned to a bookcase and reached for a folder which was full of music sheets. He drew one out and clipped it carefully to the holder. Seeing his happiness, Maria found herself affected. She felt tears prickling her eyes. She didn't want to attract attention to herself, so she gathered up her dusters and tins of polish, and slipped quietly away. Strains of a classical tune were audible as she walked along the corridor, aware of having witnessed a special moment.

* * *

"Every Christmas, we always have the same tree," Ian told Peter. "Come with me! We'll dig it up!"

"It survives from year to year?" Maria asked.

"Something to do with being re-planted near the manure heap each time, I expect," came the reply. "It's going to be a bit boggy for digging out there but we can do it, I think. We'll have to drag it in, Peter; it's tall!"

Maria thought she would happily leave the task to Ian and Peter!

She turned her attention to the tree decorations and learned they were kept in a basket which belonged in Robert's room. Here, unlike some families, they didn't store their decorations away in an attic.

"My wife passed away at Christmas time," Robert explained. "Sometimes, it feels like it is always Christmas in my heart. Time stood still, that year."

Maria followed him and they entered the master bedroom. She was holding her breath, wondering if she would feel intrusive but it was a welcoming room with a comfortable atmosphere. There was a coal fire in a grate that was guarded with a curved, gold-coloured mesh. "So old-fashioned!" Maria thought. "It's so lovely!"

The double bed was covered with an eiderdown, deep purple in colour and there were piles of richly coloured pillows and cushions, some buttoned, some silk, others velvet, in shades of mauve, red and emerald green. The carpet was deep and patterned with roses.

There were framed photographs on the dressing table, black and white pictures of a long-ago wedding day. There was Robert with his wife, Sarah and they were smiling at each other over raised champagne glasses. A beautiful bouquet of white lilies, rosebuds, carnations and gypsophila was bound with silk ribbons of cream and gold. It lay between them on a long table covered with a smooth white cloth.

"*They are not long, the days of wine and roses …* " Robert quoted, sadly.

Stooping, he reached under the bed, pulled at the handle of a basket containing Christmas decorations and drew it out for Maria to examine. "This always stays in here," he said. "Sarah cherished the baubles because they were collected over years, and some were gifts, and some were keepsakes from foreign travel …"

Together they carried the basket and a couple of extra boxes down the stairs, and if the trip into Robert's room and the past had given Maria a lump in her throat it was worth it for Peter's expression when he was brought to join the adults again. Peter had been subjected to a good wash by his mother after the digging, and had tolerated it well enough. Now, he caught his breath with excitement when he saw the open basket with its precious contents overflowing.

Peter, Amelia and Margaret selected and fixed ornaments and draped long strands of sparkling tinsel on the dark green branches. Maria wound a length of sparkling red beads around her hand, feeling thoughtful.

"What was Sarah like?" She spoke the words aloud, and could have bitten her own tongue for risking causing distress to Robert. Was she too bold? She was fascinated by the pretty, smiling woman in the wedding photographs.

It was perfectly alright. His eyes lit up, and he leaned forward from his armchair to describe the wife whom he missed so much. Sarah had been gracious, a kind lady who made visitors feel welcome and ensured her home was a lovely place, full of the scents of polish, flowers and lavender fragranced linen in every bedroom. Robert wished they had a daughter to carry on the ways of his wife but he was proud of his son, Ian's father, who would come to visit in the New Year. He let his gaze wander and Maria noticed it lingered upon Amelia, who was holding up a spinning silver star and laughing as Peter watched her.

"We are making our tree *shiny!*" Peter said, with satisfaction.

ROBERT RIDES

Again, the weather altered. Freezing rain stopped falling and the morning air was cold but with a crisp feel. The ground was drier underfoot.

When Maria headed for the stable yard, Robert proved to be up and about, dressed for riding and keen to accompany her on an early hack. He had made up his mind.

He was very cheerful; even more content, thought Maria, than he was when they first met. He asked her to saddle Cass. The tall horse had a steady temperament. Maria got him tacked up and brought him to the mounting block in the stable yard.

"I ride *long*," declared the old man in his dignified way. She adjusted the leathers for him. She took Ed and rode alongside Robert and Cass.

"You don't want to be trotting at my age!" Robert said, although, with the barely discernible legwork of one who is practised in schooling horses, he kept Cass moving at a brisk walk. It was a chilly outing but Maria forgot her cold face and fingers as they talked.

Robert described something of his family history. The mansion, he said, had belonged to the family for over one hundred years, after his own grandfather, who was a vicar, bought the property and much of the surrounding land, too. He had lived there throughout his years of work and responsibility for the parish, but following the closure of the tiny church nearby, he decided to stay in his retirement. Congregations transferred to a larger church, where services were held by a young vicar who looked after a neighbouring parish too. The old man's interests turned to sheep farming and although he was in his later years, he employed shepherds and took a keen interest in his flocks and their management.

Robert grew up at the Manse, where his father continued to care for the land and stock. He left to study and become a doctor but later he changed course, qualified as a psychotherapist, closed general practice and returned to the Welsh border to work as a counsellor. In addition, continued farming with the support of shepherds.

"Ian did a similar thing; he worked in London for a while before he travelled, then came back to the farm."

He spoke about his brother. "When we were boys, Nigel and I used to fall out with each other all the time. We had a big age gap. Then my mother, bless her heart, said he looked up to me. He was being belligerent to hide admiration. So, I gave him a chance to do a few things with me ... ride, play polo or golf and so on. We were friends before long and have stayed on good terms always. It was years ago, when things changed.

"It is much more comfortable to get along with one's family. I enjoy having Ian around the Manse. I wish ..." At this point, diverted by a group of deer emerging from a thicket nearby, Robert pointed them out to Maria and they reined in the horses and halted to admire the scene.

When they moved on, they re-joined a track which led them away from the trees and down a gentle slope, going back towards the stables.

"Come on then!" Robert exclaimed unexpectedly! He sent Cass forward in to a lively, rocking canter. Maria followed on the very willing Ed.

In the stable yard, Robert dismounted, using the block again. He handed the reins over to Maria, who had been trying to think of a way to assure him that she would take care of both the horses without sounding as if she thought he couldn't manage it. There was no need to worry, since he followed his habit and convention and was happy to leave Cass with her, in her role as groom. He unbuckled his ancient riding cap, tucked his crop beneath his arm, and wandered away, moving a fraction stiffly but looking happy.

Indoors, Maria found Margaret in the kitchen. Standing at the table, she was showing Peter how to peel a handful of Brussels sprouts.

"I take the leaves off!" Peter announced when Maria walked into the room. "Auntie Margaret cuts the stalks!"

"You're helpful, Peter!" Maria laughed. Then, to Margaret, she went on. "Did you see Robert after his ride? I stayed back to see to the horses but I wonder if I should take him a drink?"

"I saw him come in," Margaret reassured her. "He looked so happy! It's wonderful that he enjoyed a ride out like that! He's gone to have a hot bath; I expect he'll settle by his bedroom fireplace now. You don't need to worry; I put a coffee tray up there for him, with a plate of sandwiches. I expect he'll sleep in front of the fire; he's fine, just tired."

* * *

That evening, all was very quiet. Robert had remained in his suite of rooms, where Margaret continued to find him perfectly well but determined to rest. He ate supper there, by himself except for his dogs. Ian, too, was closeted into his private rooms, working. The women ate their meal with Nigel and small Peter, whose carefully prepared sprouts were duly admired alongside a tasty meat pie and baked potatoes.

"You work so hard!" Nigel told his wife. "You should have a break!"

Amelia and Maria backed him up. "Let's walk down the road to the pub!"

Margaret demurred at first, saying she loved to cook, but the younger women liked the idea of an outing and she let herself be persuaded to go with them. They left Nigel in charge of putting Peter to bed and it was a happy arrangement. First, the little boy led the way to the library to choose a storybook, with Nigel following, holding the blue teddy bear and a cup of warm milk.

Dressed in their warmest coats, Amelia, Maria and Margaret made their way towards the village on foot. A small torch was tucked into Margaret's pocket along with her mobile phone and a key, so they could be sure to re-enter the mansion on their return.

In the pub, Maria, Margaret and Amelia sat on high stools and ordered white wine. The landlady, whose name was Sally, greeted Margaret affectionately and chatted, asking in an interested way after Peter's wellbeing and sharing comments with Amelia about the local school and its teachers.

"I can go a bit spaced out after just one glass of wine," confessed Maria. "It's strange, I'll have some and notice nothing different most times, then there are others when I'll go slightly out of it!"

"A typical migraine sufferer," Margaret said wisely. "It's a funny thing. Food, too. Either not enough or an unusual combination can do it … set off the headache or sleepiness, I mean."

"Yes," Maria agreed. "Some people swear it's due to stress but that's not my trigger at all." She sipped her drink. "I ate so much dinner, I think I'll be fine, this time!"

"Let's hope so!" Margaret agreed. "You've lined your stomach!"

Sue and Jackie were seated at a small table across the room drinking sparkling wine and eating crisps. This time, it was Amelia who spotted that they cast unfriendly glances at Maria. Returning from a brief visit to the toilets, she saw their expressions. She crossed the polished floor behind the tables to join Margaret and Maria. "What's the matter with those two?" She lowered her voice, settling back onto her stool at the bar. "Maria, do you know the shop-assistants look at you as if you are an alien?"

Sally was still nearby, tidying the counter. She overheard this comment. She observed that *she* knew the reason for the unfriendly stares. Perhaps she was a little cheeky, to join in unexpectedly but the women couldn't resist her words! Leaning close together, they indulged in a spot of illuminating gossip.

* * *

In July the previous year, a garden party was held in the grounds of the mansion. Many local people who had some connection with the family were invited. Staff from the pub attended, the local dairy farmer and his wife, shepherds and their families, two gardeners who were employed by Robert to take care of the grounds in summer and many others, all went to enjoy a feast of sandwiches, strawberries and cake, and in addition to the food there were outdoor tables loaded with wine and beer.

The ladies from the village shop were included among the guests and dressed themselves up tremendously for the occasion. They met Ian and were both immediately infatuated, a fact they had not troubled to conceal when they socialised in the pub subsequently! For his part, Ian didn't succumb to the charms of either one.

"And then, along came Maria, with her wonderful hair and those eyes! Well, they're jealous!" She paused, considering this before she went on. "In fact, Amelia, once they realise you are staying in Ian's household, they'll hate you too!"

Amelia grinned, looking relaxed and Maria thought how nice it was to see her expression, so changed from the shy, anxious one she wore at the start of her stay in Robert's household. She had regained her self-confidence.

"Well, I understand what has been happening much better now, so thank you," said Maria. Sitting straighter, she felt as if something was over and done with.

"Don't worry about it," advised Sally, briskly. "My goodness, there's no need to let those two sillies get you down!"

"She has just got away from a jealous le … les … uh, I mean, *person*!" Amelia explained.

"Yes!" Maria couldn't help smiling at her friend's struggle with political correctness. "Why do people make assumptions like that? I was never going to challenge Phyllis and I'm certainly not going after Ian! I do hate it when people are angry with me for just existing!"

"Poor thing!" Sally winked at Margaret. She began to clear empty glasses from the bar.

Amelia was watching Maria's face. "You do like Ian?"

"He can be charming," said Maria. "He's often funny. I already told him; he reminds me of my brother, though!" The assertion, which began as a lie, was still untrue but Maria wanted to avoid confusing Amelia. The fact was, she was fairly affectionate towards Ian now, and he certainly could make her laugh. Possibly, these were sisterly emotions and yet they didn't really match her feelings.

"Perhaps …" (she amended the thought privately, wondering if she was inventing her own new word) "… we're *cousinly*!"

Margaret's Kitchen

Christmas Day was approaching and Margaret had begun to lay plans for the festive meal. As all cooks who prepare for the big day know, it can be a taxing process, especially as life continues normally ahead of the festivities and the household must eat!

For a midday meal of hot sausage rolls, garlic baguettes and salad, Margaret called the group to the big table in the kitchen. If everyone ate their lunch at the same time, she explained, she could clear the surfaces afterwards and do some Christmas baking!

Peter was sent to fetch Robert from the library and they came to the table holding hands, each one as keen to eat as the other. Robert enjoyed his meals and seemed well able to indulge his spare frame. Peter climbed into his chair at the table and he had a piece of information to impart to Maria. "I'm growing! That's what Amelia says!"

His mother had just entered the room and headed for the kitchen sink to wash her hands before the meal. She began to make a juice drink for her small son and corrected him, with a smile. "I think you mean, *Mum!*"

* * *

To begin her afternoon of baking, Margaret said she would make mince pies. Even though they had barely eaten lunch, the room had darkened and lights were switched on. Through the windows, a few flakes of snow could be seen, drifting from the sky. When the adults pointed them out to Peter, he obediently stood for a few moments, to stare through the glass, before turning back to the interesting task he'd been given. With a silvery collection of pastry cutters in a variety of shapes, the little boy perched on two cushions placed on a kitchen chair and was soon pressing the metal shapes carefully into floury dough. He cut lots of circles, then progressed to making stars and holly leaves.

Maria washed her hands, poured tea from the pot which Margaret always kept hot and fresh, then sat beside the little boy. She showed him how to add more flour when the pastry got sticky but was soon assigned a task of her own: scooping sweet mincemeat from a jar, to dab into the pie bases. The dogs went under the table near her feet, where they leaned affectionately, hoping for pastry scraps. When Jaff stood up to push his way out from beneath the tablecloth, he jogged her elbow, which resulted in a dollop of mincemeat landing on his massive head and a burst of laughter from Peter.

Maria had something she wanted to ask Amelia. "Peter said you had certificates?"

Amelia was standing at the sink, washing up the lunch time crockery. She tried to laugh off the question. "Oh, well …!"

Maria persisted. "When you played the piano? You know how to play, and Robert was so pleased! Have you got lots of musical training?"

At last, Amelia had to admit it. She was musically gifted.

* * *

The household was vibrant with people and Robert remarked often that he liked it! As a rule, he was there with just Ian for company and his housekeeper for part of each day. The Christmas preparations included himself and Ian of course, along with Margaret and Nigel, and Maria, Amelia and Peter. Everyone was conscious that Margaret had given herself a good deal of work to do, when she appointed herself the person in charge of the kitchen! By mutual consent, they offered to help her whenever they could.

Once Maria had changed her clothes after horse duties, she began to make a habit of returning downstairs, especially to share in kitchen duties. Margaret didn't argue, and always found tasks to hand to her helpers.

New linen for the dining room table was needed one morning and Maria walked swiftly past the sitting room doorway, glimpsing the comfortable room and Robert, who was in his usual armchair near a freshly lit fire. In between the kitchen and the warm room across the passageway, there were scents of apple wood and fresh coffee in the air. She went up a narrow flight of stairs which was tucked behind a latched door adjacent to the porch. She could reach the vast airing cupboard, this way. After she had loaded her arms with a pristine tablecloth and some matching serviettes, she returned by the main staircase.

She passed the small study which both Robert and Ian sometimes used, heard the thud of a fallen book and an exclamation. Then, Ian's voice stated loudly to someone (perhaps on the telephone) "*I just haven't got time!*"

Margaret was seated at the kitchen table and in front of her was a freshly washed cutlery tray and a heap of silver. She was polishing knives, forks and spoons and sorting them into the tray. Maria put the folded tablecloth and the tea towels on the table.

"Thank you! Do you want a cup of tea?"

Maria hesitated. "I might come back and get one soon," she answered. "Thanks … but I heard Ian in the study just now. I wonder if I could help him; he seemed to be getting a bit wound up about something!"

Margaret looked doubtful. "He is usually well organised," she said. "Although, I have heard him saying that paperwork holds him up sometimes, now I think about it! You could offer help and see what happens!"

"I'll take him a cup of tea," Maria decided. "If he seems to want to stay on his own, I can leave him to it!"

"Take coffee," Margaret advised. "Ian isn't one for tea, except in the afternoon!"

So, Maria filled a gold rimmed coffee cup and carried it, rattling a little on its saucer as she made her way back along the passage to the study, where the door remained ajar. There were documents scattered across the desktop and a laptop was open but the screen was blank. Ian was leaning back in his swivel chair. He looked around at Maria.

"Coffee?" She stepped into the room.

"Oh, great!" He sat straighter and accepted the cup and saucer. "I keep losing the internet connection … and I've lost a hard copy of something … it's here, somewhere!" He indicated the pile of papers with an impatient gesture. His dark hair was on end and Maria thought he looked as if he had been running his hands through it.

"I've finished outside," she told him. "The horses are okay and the dogs are with Robert. Can I help?"

"I must admit, I've got to the point where I can't make sense of this lot!" Ian admitted. "If you really have an hour to spare, could you tidy it up? If I tell you what the missing document looks like, maybe you can find it?" He stood up and gave her his seat, and she slid into it and turned her attention to the task.

"It's got a waxed seal on the front," Ian said helpfully. "A red one. My brain's got tired but I know it's in there, somewhere!" He stooped to stir glowing coals in the grate with a poker. A handful of dry twigs, which he snapped and added to the fire, crackled as they caught light. He closed the door, before settling himself into the easy chair with a sigh of relief. A clock on the bookcase could be heard, faintly ticking.

They were companionable, as Maria turned her attention to her task and Ian remained thoughtful. Fresh to the problem, Maria wasn't over faced by the quantity of sheets of paper that needed sorting. She saw they were a mixture of accounts sheets and letters. Soon she had separated the two and then she carefully put each block into date order. In doing so, after about twenty minutes she had found the lost pages, closely typed and stapled together, bearing the red seal in a corner of the top sheet.

Ian had remained quiet, drinking his coffee.

Maria twisted around in her chair and held up the document. "Oh!" He leaned towards her and took it gratefully. "Yes, that's the one!" He stood up, opened a drawer in the desk, and found a new folder.

Maria stood up, too. "That's good," she said. "I'll go and help Margaret now!" The leather topped desk looked well-ordered.

"You really made a difference, Maria!" Ian said. "I don't know what's the matter with me; I hardly ever lose important things! What will I do without you, when January comes?" He meant to be jovial, asking a rhetorical question, nothing more. Instead, coupled with his confession that he was struggling to keep on top of his work, the words sounded heartfelt and as soon as they were said, he seemed to realise it. He shrugged. He couldn't take them back.

Maria decided to treat the comment as if its only meaning could be casual. "Get a secretary?" She smiled and for a moment he grinned with his more typical, cheery air. Somehow (Maria reflected, later), the moment stretched itself. As Ian continued to look down at her face without answering, there was a silence while they regarded one another.

Maria didn't want to be involved in meaningful silences and gazes! She shook her head, collected the empty cup and escaped to the peaceful kitchen and Margaret's calm company.

Mixing It Up

Peter continued to refer to his mother by her Christian name. He was a dignified little boy, and as an only child he never heard anyone else refer to her as mum or mother. Amelia thought it didn't matter, as long as he wasn't cheeky; nevertheless, gently, she made sure to correct him. "*Mum,* actually …"

On an evening when the storm outside caused everyone to seek comfort indoors at the fireside an hour earlier than usual, the group gathered in the long sitting room and enjoyed the warmth of a blazing fire. Robert had switched on an extra lamp which stood on his side table by his favourite chair, and he frowned over a crossword puzzle in his newspaper. Peter liked to be close to Robert, where he was supplied with a folded newspaper of his own, and made careful marks and a few legible words on the pages with his pencil.

Nigel stood at the French windows. He had pulled the drapes open a few inches so he could watch the storm while he sipped his brandy.

"You make me feel chilly," complained Margaret from her seat at the largest circular table in the room, where she sat, working on a jigsaw puzzle with Maria and Amelia. "Shut the curtains, Nigel!"

"When I look at the cold scene out there, I feel warm in here!" Nigel told his wife. He pulled the tasselled cord to shut the drapes and went to sit in his usual armchair.

Ian walked across the room from the drink cabinet carrying two glasses of red wine. "A day without wine ..." he said, contentedly, "... is like a day without the sun."

"Meal!" Robert mentioned, putting a hand out to receive his glass.

"Huh?" Ian placed his glass on the mantle shelf above the fire and went back to the cabinet to pour white wine for Maria and Margaret.

"It's *a meal* ..." Robert took a sip. *"A meal without wine ..."*

Peter drew a circle and added some rays: it was a picture of the sun. He sat back on his heels and contemplated his pencilled scribbles and his drawing. *"A meal without wine,"* he repeated. *"Amelia* without wine ..."

The grown-ups smiled but there was more to come when, in his childish tones he announced: "A day without Amelia, is like a day without the sun!"

"Now you've mixed it up!" Robert told him.

Maria shared an amused glance with her friend. "Your child is so bright!"

Ian took a swallow of red wine. He swirled the remainder of the drink in the glass, looking at the boy with a thoughtful expression.

* * *

Maria was very careful to feed Boy and Jaff exactly the quantities and types of food specified by Robert. Like many dog owners, he was particular about the animals' diet.

They were given a mixture of meaty tinned food and plain biscuits. Unsalted, cooked vegetables could be added when there were leftovers available from the dinner table, and scraps of roasted chicken or lamb but these must be substituted for tinned meat, not added to it. The dogs must not have pork *ever* and they were not given dried mixtures produced and sold for dogs.

"It's not proper dog food," said Robert. He was irritable about it. "The only people who promote that disgusting, concentrated stuff are the ones who stand to make money out of it. I'm not surprised it makes Boy go off his head, so I won't give it to him. It shortens the lives of many dogs! When will people realise their dog never needed to get ill?"

Maria knew she was obliged to feed the dogs on the diet chosen by their owner, regardless of her own feelings about their best interests but she was profoundly relieved to be shown supplies of good quality tinned food, plain mixer biscuits. It was good to be given the freedom to add a spoonful of cooked vegetables or stew occasionally. She had met far too many dogs whose early enthusiasm for the highly flavoured pellets led to them being given the stuff on a daily basis, and she knew this could cause loss of appetite and even kidney disorders or fits. She was in perfect agreement with Robert.

Boy had a touch of arthritis in his hind legs and to ease discomfort he was sometimes given special pills, usually just one each day. Maria had discovered that administering this important pill was far more difficult than one would expect! The dog spotted the pill in his dish no matter how carefully it was hidden and often he would lick around the offending medicine until it remained, a soggy blob when everything that tasted good was eaten. If it was crushed into the food and stirred, he left the whole lot. Maria had developed a way of pressing the pill into a cube of cheese, which she then rolled in her hand and pretended she was about to eat. "Yum!"

With Boy's interested attention then, she would show this to him in her palm, whereupon the offering became an acceptable treat and he ate it quickly, in a gulp. (Jaff, who was jealous, would have gobbled up the pill regardless of how it was presented, so he was given a small cube of cheese too!)

One afternoon, preparing the dogs' supper with the pair closely at her feet, Maria was called out of the kitchen by Margaret, who wanted to show her a news item on the television. She left open tins, a bag of cereal-based dog biscuit and a single red pill on the worktop. When she returned after barely two minutes, the pill had disappeared and Maria wondered (as one can when an action is the same, performed every day) if she imagined leaving it there!

Upon counting those remaining in the foil-wrapped slip, it was clear she had definitely removed the one she was about to give the dog. Peter was sitting at the table, surrounded by scattered felt-tipped pens, carefully outlining a sketch of a car, drawn for him by Ian. Maria decided quickly what she would do and she hurried to find Robert. She confided that Peter might have eaten Boy's pill. Did she need to be worried, if so?

"The main thing," observed Robert in a considered fashion, from behind his newspaper, "is to ensure the dog has enough tablets to last the week."

"Peter?"

"Peter will be fine."

Maria believed in Robert's judgment, knowing he was once a well-respected general practitioner but she was still considering her duties as she hurried back to the kitchen. She must tell Amelia, surely, just to be on the safe side regarding her son's health but also, there was the delicate question of tackling Peter about what he seemed to have done. He was not the sort of child who normally took a treat (he must have thought the pill was a sweet, she reasoned) without asking first.

"So," her anxious mind went on worrying in the space of less than a minute, as she left the sitting room and crossed the hallway. "There's the taking of it and then there's the danger of unknown medicines! Shall I have a quiet word, or tell his mother?"

However, the panic was soon over. Peter looked up from his drawings. "Where did you go, Maria? I was going to tell you I moved that tablet for Boy, in case Jaff ate it!" He bent his head over his work again. "That dog is so tall!"

Maria was so relieved she had to turn away, to lean against the worktop for a moment, with her legs shaking and a private smile to hide. "You are a very grown-up boy!" she told Peter. "Thank you!"

GIFTS

Present-giving might be something of a muddle, they realised. There had been no post or parcel deliveries because of the snow in the village and the surrounding lanes.

Since Margaret had arrived at the Manse at Robert's invitation, expressly to share the Christmas period with him, she had a collection of items in a special case and they were intended as gifts. She had expected Mrs Moss to be there, so, with characteristic kindness, she had included toiletries scented with lavender and violets. When Amelia worried about gifts for Peter, Margaret offered a sparkling bath bomb, a small yellow plastic duck which had been packaged inside a gift set for adults, just for fun, and a jar full of marshmallow sweets. They could make some playdough, Amelia realised, using kitchen store cupboard ingredients of flour, oil and food colouring. A chocolate Father Christmas was discovered in in boxed collection of items which had arrived in a goodwill gesture, a gift for Robert and Ian from the local shop.

Amelia was relieved and all the adults felt the same.

"The only person who needs everything to be just right is Peter!" Margaret insisted. Nevertheless, she disappeared by herself into the dining room on Christmas Eve, carrying bulging carrier bags, rolls of gift-wrap and sticky tape as well as silk ribbons and a bundle of pens. She had such a store of new fragrances and unopened bath oils; she easily found some things suitable to give the two younger women.

Next to take over the room and close herself inside privately, to wrap her son's gifts on top of the long table, was Amelia and finally in went Robert, being mysterious. Ian explained that his grandfather always placed small parcels beside each dinner plate on Xmas Day and he would have a little hoard of chocolates and luxury soaps, to draw from.

* * *

The family would eat their meal on Christmas Day at one o'clock. "It's a tradition we never change," Robert explained. "And we drink Buck's Fizz in the morning!"

Margaret sat close to his armchair by the hearth in the sitting room, leaning forward with her notebook resting on her knee and an attentive air. She made notes, written in a beautiful flowing hand. They discussed the dishes he wanted her to serve, and after the traditional favourite were in place, Robert thoughtfully invited others in the room to make suggestions.

"Pigs-in-blankets!" Nigel said. "Must have those!"

"We've got them written down, dear," was Margaret's calm reply.

Maria said she like almonds mixed in with the brussels sprouts. Ian wanted a Yorkshire pudding even though he knew it wasn't really the thing with Christmas dinner.

"Sausages!" offered Peter.

"Yes," Margaret said again, kindly. "We have those covered!" She had placed herself unequivocally in charge of the food preparations although she assigned and delegated jobs happily. It was quite possible to remember she was a trained nurse, used to ordering others about!

As the others around the fireside drank tea and listened, each was given their task. Nigel was to prepare vegetables. Peter could make the pigs-in-blankets and help to set the table. Maria would boil potatoes and mash them with butter and cream, and also make sure the gravy was well-stirred and did not burn. Amelia planned to sit at the table with Peter and make stuffing balls. Ian, decided Margaret, could fill the heated trolley with hot dishes to wheel it into the dining-room and at the right time, he was to make the pudding flame.

Plans fell into place and Maria could imagine how enjoyable the shared meal would be. Champagne would be served, as well as red and white wines, and lemonade for Peter; there would be a fresh cream trifle for those who were not so keen on the rich pudding, or anyone who had space for two desserts! Silver dishes of chocolates would be on the drink cabinet, to be brought to the table after they finished the meal itself.

"I'm looking forward to it," Amelia said. "I'm so grateful to be here!"

Maria gave a nod of agreement, while Margaret cast a motherly glance towards Amelia and Robert answered graciously. "We are enjoying your company, my dear."

However, there was more to all the preparations than simple pleasure in the provision of good food. Robert, leaning back with the important business of planning done, a satisfied air and an observation. "The main thing is, to create festivity *par excellence!*"

Maria thought about Elis, alone in his small croft except for his dogs and Smoke. After their planning session, she quietly asked Margaret: might he be invited to share their Christmas meal? She was diffident, knowing that the family must have its own traditions, and perhaps a shepherd who kept himself very isolated (by choice, apparently) wasn't someone to recommend as a guest.

Could Elis join in with the household that day, or would he stay by himself? Maria wanted to know, and Margaret received her questions without showing any sign of surprise.

"Well, he will," she said. "I mean, he *will* stay on his own. We can invite him and actually, I know Robert and Ian always make sure they do. But he stays quiet."

It didn't seem right, but once the invitation was extended and declined, then clearly pressing Elis to come to share a festive dinner could embarrass him. She learned that every year, it was Robert, who took it upon himself to walk up to the croft to talk with Elis.

Maria's mind strayed a little. It occurred to her that Nigel and Margaret were annual visitors. They were used to Robert's Christmas traditions. She remembered his surprise, followed swiftly by a well-mannered recovery, when it seemed he had forgotten they were coming that day! Certainly, Margaret had referred to their early arrival when everyone had to decide how to manage without Mrs Moss. Now, she mentioned it again.

"We are here sooner than usual this year," she said. "Maybe Nigel will go up with Robert this time, and put a bit of emphasis on the invitation!"

"Could do." Nigel was listening to the conversation as he sat near the Aga, shining up a pair of leather boots. "Might be better for two to go, now Rob' is getting near eighty! I know he often comes home with a fair drop of something inside him! Sherry, or brandy. They are good friends." He was doubtful about the invitation however. "I'd guess Elis will still refuse to come down for dinner."

"It seems very stubborn of him!" Maria couldn't stop herself from letting the comment escape!

"Got to be respectful," was Nigel's ambiguous reply.

* * *

So, it seemed that Elis would stay all by himself. Maria knew it must be a deliberate choice; yet, to do that even over Christmas seemed to reflect some kind of pointless self-denial and she found it hard to bear.

"Robert does, always, go to visit Elis during the week before Christmas," Maria was told when she revisited the subject. "I don't think he's ever failed to do that. Sometimes he takes the Land

Rover. Often, he rides Cass, with Abe alongside on Ed."

They had never been prevented from the visit, because of bad weather? No, never. If snow or rain made it impossible to ride horses or drive uphill, then Robert dressed in warm layers of clothing, donned heavy boots, and walked.

Respectfully, Maria asked Robert if she could go with him this year. He seemed agreeable, and confirmed they would walk the route because the snowy weather meant there would be no ride this year. "It's a long trek," he admitted. "But we'll put a drop of something in my hip flask and tog ourselves up, and we'll do it!"

Maria supposed that Ian might go if Robert could not, but nothing was said to that effect. She thought Robert seemed quite keen on the idea of braving the weather to make the trip! She was aware of an interested glance from Margaret but she was genuinely motivated by a wish to ensure the elderly gentleman took care on the way there and when he returned home. For sure, she also hoped a mild comment from herself might sway the decision of the farmer, to alter his habitual isolation and join them at their Christmas table.

When they set out, a layer of snow on the hillside made sure their decision not to ride was sensible. However, they needed to take care of themselves and they wore layers of warm clothing, with scarves, mittens and hats so that every extremity was protected. Maria put her mobile phone into her pocket and Robert prudently tucked a gentleman's silver flask full of brandy inside his coat. He wore the kind of furry hat that has ear flaps, and stood patiently while Margaret tied a neat bow beneath his chin. Maria wore a woollen bobble hat. It was possible to walk along the route because a snow plough made a daily trip to free a pathway for farmers.

Maria had made up her mind to ask Robert a question, although she planned that if he was diffident or unhappy about it, she would change the subject. They set off, crunching over icy snow, and feeling their cheeks becoming cold at once. But Robert was able to walk quite well on his long legs, and they kept up a good pace. Soon she asked, had there been an argument between Ian and Elis? She assumed the two men were once friends who fell out for some reason, although the farmer soon showed up to visit when he heard about Ian's fall. Robert didn't seem to be offended, and in just a few words he explained that (so far as he could tell) the pair generally seemed to rub each other up the wrong way. "A pity …" was his only expression of his own feelings about that.

"Elis won't come for dinner," she said, realising it was a fact, as they trudged and talked.

"No. He never does, but I always ask him. It's a Christmas gift, of sorts."

* * *

At the croft, Robert and Maria were confronted with a swiftly opened door, two excited dogs, and Elis himself, who courteously invited them to enter. Robert was shown to the most comfortable chair by the hearth at once, while Maria stooped, pulling at knots in her bootlaces.

She heard the white cat, mewing and complaining beneath the front window of the building and, without considering her action at all, she unlatched and opened the door. At once, the cat ran in, carrying a live mouse in his jaws.

"*Smoke!*" She grabbed him, halting his progress. Lifted a few inches from the floor, he dropped his captive into her palm. Not a mouse but a furious shrew, the tiny thing bit her very hard, on the thumb of her left hand.

"Oh, *flip!*" Maria let go of the cat with her right hand and, with an involuntary gesture due to the pain, sent the shrew spinning out through the open doorway. It landed unharmed in the soft snow on the path outside, plunged into the bank and disappeared.

Smoke stalked towards the fireplace.

"Ow!" Maria went to hold her sore thumb under the cold tap at the sink, running icy water over a small wound.

Elis opened a cupboard and reaching inside, he withdrew a plastic box and removed the lid. "Let me take a look?"

He glanced at her hand as she washed away a thin stream of blood, then he snipped a strip of sticking plaster from a new roll and turned to rummage in the bottom of the container. When he looked up, she saw he was grinning broadly!

"Why are you laughing?" Maria demanded crossly.

He shook his head. His eyes were still creased at the corners.

"No, why are you …?"

"*What* did you say, when that thing got you?"

"Nothing at all," she lied defensively. In something of a non sequitur, she went on. "Anyway, shrews bite harder than mice!"

"They do." Elis agreed. He unscrewed the lid of the tube of ointment. "Of course, you would yell!" He turned off the running water and took her hand in his own. "Flip," he repeated. "Is that what you said?"

"Well," Maria frowned at her sore thumb as he applied a thick cotton pad to dry it, then some antiseptic gel and a piece of sticking plaster. "I don't swear!"

"She doesn't!" Robert was amused by their exchange. "She's a good lass." He sipped from a crystal glass full of sherry, patting the heads of the dogs, both having left their usual spot on the fireside rug to vie with one another for the closest place beside him.

Once she was doctored to Elis' satisfaction and freed, Maria gathered Smoke into her arms. "He bears me no grudge for spoiling his fun!"

The two men talked about the farm and the stock for perhaps forty minutes. They completed their small business when Robert asked his question. "Will you come to dinner, on Christmas Day?"

The younger man, as expected, declined. "Thank you, sir. I'm happy to stay here."

It was an old-fashioned exchange, Maria thought, and it sounded well-rehearsed. And yet, even though the idea was illogical considering Margaret's explanations too, she couldn't help wondering whether she had a part in this scenario. *Is he holding back because of me?* She stared into the flickering fire.

Margaret had explained that Elis always remained on his own over Christmas, and she had made this sound definite. However, she had also advised that it was possible the farmer would not risk getting in the way of Ian's interest in Maria, perhaps because he would imagine Ian had a prior claim on her affections since she was employed at the Manse. Cuddling the purring, furry bundle that was Elis' forgiving cat, she waited for Robert to decide it was time to leave,

Robert, innocent of any grudge, shook hands with Elis. Then he took his coat and shrugged into it with the younger man's help, donned again his scarf and heavy mittens and covered his head with his fur hat. Maria saw he left the strings loose, but she hadn't Margaret's sense of familiarity and didn't step forward to tie them up. She hoped the hat wouldn't fly from his head, in the wind. They stepped from the doorway into swirling snow and began the march downhill in amicable silence.

Did it disappoint the old man when Elis declined the invitation to share dinner on Christmas Day? If so, he was very patient, thought Maria. For his part, Robert did not comment about the friendship that had clearly developed between herself and Elis, or wonder aloud whether she herself might be disappointed by that stubborn self-exclusion.

Robert halted after all, to remove his mittens and secure his hat strings for himself. Then he pulled the mittens on his hands again, while Maria dug her gloved hands deeply into her coat pockets. Robert took her arm and thus, with no further comment but companionably linked, they made their way home.

Taking Care

On a day when the snow was whirling into the air in flurries, Maria decided not to ride. Instead, she spent extra time on grooming Ed and Cass, working with dandy and body brushes until their coats shone, before replacing their rugs. When stable chores were completed, she made her way back into the house. She was reproaching herself for failing to prepare her usual early snack of mixed fruits, since this omission could lead to a fall in blood sugars and a headache. Today, she had been too hasty in going across to the stables. She had even left her little pouch full of sweets in her room.

Like many migraine sufferers, Maria occasionally forgot or abandoned the routine she needed to follow in order to avoid an attack. Inevitably, sometimes she regretted it. Sure enough, she was, as she informed Margaret, going "a bit floaty".

"You started very early today!" Margaret commented. "I noticed your boots and coat had gone when I was about to get my breakfast! Sit yourself by the Aga, Maria."

After depositing her burden in the great hearth, she returned and began to make porridge. "Honey or brown sugar?" They were chatting, sharing dietary ideas, when Ian arrived in the kitchen to pour his coffee.

"You look very pale," he told Maria, in passing. She guessed she had lost her colour since her head was beginning to ache and the porridge, welcome though it was, had not forestalled a migraine. She stood up, placed her empty dish on the counter and lost her balance. "Whoops!" He was right beside her, and caught her in his arms.

"Bed for you!" Margaret ordered. "What kind of medicine do you usually take?"

"I've got painkillers," Maria said. "There are some tablets in the bedside drawer. I'll just need water please, Margaret."

Ian supported Maria, with one of his arms wrapped firmly around her waist and a hand holding hers. She laid her palm against his, feeling glad of his help. Together, they walked up the stairs and along the upper passageway. Margaret hurried ahead, walking flat-footed and fast in the manner of a trained nurse, carrying a glass of water and saying she would turn down the bedcovers.

"My eyes are whirling!" Maria complained.

Ian chuckled. "Well, they aren't, so far as I can tell …"

Amelia emerged from her room with Peter behind her. "Hey," she greeted them. Margaret had already passed her door but Ian and Maria were coming along much more slowly.

"I can't really see you!" Maria told her.

"She's gone weird," Ian said helpfully.

"Headache," Maria added, but that was all she said because her lips were numb.

"Poor Maria!" Amelia said, kindly.

Peter was about to run along the corridor but he mentioned that he would probably come to read to her, after he finished his breakfast. "That," commented Ian, "is a nice idea, but maybe best for later on. Can you wait until she's had a sleep, first?"

The child nodded. "It's sausages," he said, still on the subject of his breakfast. "I'm having lots of red sauce!" He tore off, with Amelia hastening behind him.

Ian saw the expression on Maria's face. "Don't think about that!" He smiled down at her. "I know how migraine makes people feel because my mother gets the same thing."

Margaret had prepared Maria's bedcovers as promised, and also thoughtfully closed curtains to darken the room. In the dim light Maria collapsed gratefully onto the bed, with her head spinning. She kicked off her indoor shoes, Ian lifted her ankles to make her comfortable, and covered her with the quilt. Then he patted her shoulder and left.

In a moment, Maria raised herself on her elbow to find a box of painkillers in the drawer of a small unit beside her, swallowed two with water and then closed her eyes and fell into a deep sleep.

When she awoke, the little clock on her dresser showed that two hours had passed. She felt slightly better and sat up to drink water. Her room felt warm and safe, and the sounds of a storm outside only seemed to increase her sense of comfort. She was conscious that she had been dreaming, confusedly, that Elis was patting her shoulder and Amelia was asking her something, but the words weren't clear.

* * *

Ian spent a whole day by himself, closeted inside his private study where he worked on   creating spreadsheets for the farm accounts. He emerged only a couple of times, to make a sandwich or pour coffee from the cafetiere. At the end of the afternoon, he announced he was going stir crazy from being shut in, and loopy from drinking nothing but coffee or water. If anyone cared to accompany him to the pub, the drinks were on him!

In this invitation, he had several takers and before long, warmly dressed, everyone except Robert (who said he would read a book and keep an ear open for Peter) and Peter (who was peacefully sleeping in his bed) marched with Ian along the track that wound downhill to the village.

The public house was well-lit and its heated, convivial atmosphere was welcome after their chilly walk. It was full of customers but the group found a cushioned corner seat and drew up some chairs too. In accordance with Ian's instructions, each one ordered what he or she fancied and soon the round, polished table in front of them was cluttered with an array of glasses. Considering her recent headache, Maria chose lemonade.

Margaret and Amelia fell into a murmured conversation with each other. Nigel wandered over to the fireside, to chat to a couple who had recognised him and were beckoning to him.

Ian took a great swallow of his drink and sat back in his seat. He was already on his second beer, having drained the first while the barman assembled their tray. Since they were all on foot with no need for a driver, he had relaxed.

Maria sipped her drink, but she eyed Ian with slight mistrust. He was looking rather bright-eyed. He caught her glance and grinned. "It's nice and warm, in here!"

She nodded. "My feet are thawing nicely!"

"It's not very warm, up at the croft!"

She was right; he was looking for trouble! Despite having guessed it, Maria fell into the little trap. "Oh, I don't agree! It's very cosy!"

Her few words were intended to be dismissive but they fell from her lips with some kind of importance. Ian regarded her as if she had said something startling. She caught his expression, saw the raised eyebrows and found herself becoming self-conscious. She felt as if she had said something revealing! Foolishly, she ploughed on.

"I mean, it's not a bit cold with the fire … you know …"

Her comment tailed off. She could only make this worse, if she tried to explain herself! She had taken the bait and risen to the defence of Elis' lifestyle.

Nigel, returning to their table, overheard Maria's comment. He agreed, thinking she referred to the glowing coals in the fireplace nearby. "Aye, it's a good fire!"

Margaret and Amelia were ready to join in with the rest of their group, and Ian seized the opportunity to be difficult. "Do you know?" he began expansively. "I really think Maria has the most beautiful eyes in ..." he paused momentarily, then finished with "the village!"

This was something of a back-handed compliment, since the village was tiny. Maria glowered but he grinned affably and raised his glass to her with a nod. He was being sly.

Sweet-natured Amelia was loyal to her friend. She corrected the comment. "The best eyes," she said, "... in the *county!*"

Margaret frowned. She was glad Amelia could join in with the joke but she saw the situation in a serious light. Ian had been spending time with the young woman, who was looking happier as a result.

Margaret happened to be seated next to her nephew, and she was the only one who overheard one more mumbled addition to the exchange when he lowered his chin, brought his glass to his lips and said, *"or the world ... "*

* * *

As their party made their way back uphill, Ian felt in his pockets and declared he was not sure where the door key was. No-one had brought their mobile phone with them. They began to hurry, hoping Robert had not gone to bed, somehow already feeling colder because they feared they would not be able to get inside the mansion.

When the party arrived before the great doorway, it swung open just as they started to deliberate about whether or not the back door might still be unlocked. Robert was ready to let them in; he had spotted Ian's key still in its place on a hook in the hallway. Relieved they crowded inside, where Ian offered to make coffee for everyone. Maria went with Nigel to join Robert, who had returned at once to the warm fireside in the sitting room but Amelia excused herself and said she would check on her son and then go to bed.

In the kitchen, Ian filled and switched on the kettle before perching on the edge of the chair by the Aga, where he pulled his boots from cold feet, grumbling about frozen toes.

Margaret placed cups on a tray, then went to sit in front of him, drawing up a chair and leaning forward with an air of determination.

It was a moment before Ian looked up and realised how close she was, and how focused on him. He looked at her uneasily. "That's your nurse's face, Auntie," he said.

"It *is* my serious face," she agreed. "Ian, we all know you're a charmer. I don't want to see broken hearts here this Christmas, or wrecked happiness, before we all go home. It's been lovely so far, in some very unexpected ways. When you said what you did about Maria and her pretty eyes …"

"Hah!" Ian was relieved; he placed his hands on the arms of his chair and made as if to rise. "I shouldn't have drunk those beers so fast! Bless you, she didn't care. She gives me a hard time too!"

"I'm not worried about Maria," Margaret answered, reaching out to touch his arm, pressing gently. He sighed and sat down. "She is strong and I think, *sisterly* towards you!"

"Sisterly?" Ian repeated the word as if he felt surprised but he didn't argue. He leaned back with a lazy movement and became reflective. "Hm."

"I want you to treat Amelia respectfully!" When Margaret saw she had his attention she patted his sleeve again and went on. "I believe it matters and that's why I'm perhaps going a bit far, to say, Ian, look at *Amelia's* eyes. They tell you something!" She removed her hand and got to her feet. "Let's get this coffee going!"

She went to the refrigerator to collect a carton of milk and poured some of the contents into a small white jug, which she placed on the tray alongside matching cups. She added a rose-patterned bowl, full of brown sugar.

Ian stayed in his chair, reclining with his long legs stretched before him. He seemed pensive, stroking the silky head of Jaff, who stood amiably at his side. At length, with a sigh, he confided in his aunt. "You know what, Margaret? If only Maria *didn't* beat me up? Well, I don't mind telling you this! She would have my heart."

Margaret knew it and she liked his honesty. She remained silent. He went on speaking regretfully. "With me, she'd laugh all day. *We* would laugh. All the time."

Margaret continued to prepare their drinks, stirring hot coffee. She heard the faint pathos in his words. "Things would be less complicated, wouldn't they, if it was only Amelia who had come here this year?"

"That's true. I'd have fallen head over heels in a straightforward way! Maria is so ... different." He fell silent, not annoyed but thoughtful still.

Margaret let the conversation lapse too. Then Ian spoke again. "I feel a bit guilty ..."

At that, his aunt drew a line. "No, you shouldn't. It's an age-old situation, really! Remember too, it's not as if you are committed to either of these young women. If they both leave in a couple of weeks' time and you don't see them again, your life will go on just as before!"

Ian sighed again. He continued to fondle the dog's smooth head.

In a few minutes, Margaret's tray was ready and she spoke once more, just briefly. "Alright?"

Ian left his seat and went to her side to lift the tray, first adding a handful of teaspoons, making a clatter. "Yes, thank you, Margaret. You have said things I knew ... I think ... but also, made me see them a bit differently."

* * *

Amelia went about the mansion light footed in the silk ballet slippers given to her by Margaret. In addition to taking care of her son, she enjoyed sharing in planning meals every day, and spent much of her time in the kitchen, preparing food and cooking. For the bulk of their ingredients and supplies, Ian occasionally drove in his range rover to the local shop, after Margaret placed her orders over the telephone. Boxes full of groceries were made ready for collection.

Amelia took on her share of cleaning work, and would often be in the long room that was Robert's favourite sitting room, quietly dusting surfaces, picking up his fallen papers and books, or kneeling to sweep away spilt ash at the front of the great hearth. She was mindful of the old man's feelings and his comfort, and she shared Margaret's constant care to ensure he was well supplied with tea or coffee. She liked to sit with him, to listen to tales of times gone by.

Maria had a commitment to the horses, and could afford less time to involve herself in the daily indoor chores. She did what she could. Amelia had a love of creating a living environment that felt cosy and she genuinely enjoyed supporting Margaret, taking on many cleaning tasks. By mutual consent, the women left the men's rooms alone, reasoning that the bedrooms had already been prepared for December by the regular cleaners.

Relaxed and pretty, even a little ethereal with her gentleness and musical talent, Amelia's favourite borrowed garment was a cashmere sweater belonging to Margaret. In a shade of dusk rose, it flattered her complexion and its softness enhanced her youthful charm. She had found her place in the household. Robert became confident about asking her to play for him, and their musical hours sometimes attracted other listeners, especially Nigel, and Ian too when he had time.

She was not the sort of mother to imagine that the responsibility for Peter's happiness and welfare belonged to anyone but herself, however both Margaret and Maria enjoyed the child's company and chatter. In the stables, when he began to show an interest in joining her, Maria made sure there was always a tin of chocolate biscuits inside her freshly-cleaned cupboards.

Peter liked to settle himself alongside the dogs while she attended to the cleaning of tack. He learned how to polish the saddles until they shone. Sometimes, he brought paper and pencils and sat, drawing pictures of people riding horses.

"That's lovely!" Maria said. "Is that one a picture of me? You made my plait a mile long!"

"Heh," Peter was very good at memorising the plots in his story books. "Like *Rapunzel!*" He drew more figures clinging to long-legged horses. "There's Ian and there's Uncle Nigel …!"

Together they were content and his mother was able to have some free time.

* * *

After the child shed tears for his own toys, Ian had delved into some old trunks in his room and found a box of plastic building bricks. Robert was approving when this was brought to the fireside rug and opened for Peter, who responded with an eager exclamation. "Is that for me?" He hurried to see what Ian brought for him. Amelia quietly reminded him to say *thank you*, before they knelt together, to begin building.

On an evening following his confidential talk with Margaret, Ian selected an armchair, sat down and patiently allowed a few bricks to be arranged on his knees as Peter chattered. He let his gaze linger on Amelia, who was wearing her favourite sweater and a pair of Maria's jeans, rolled up to the knees. She sat cross-legged on the rug. Her pale curls fell over her forehead as she concentrated on her efforts and with small hands sorted the bricks into sets of large and small, for Peter. Each slim finger was tipped with bright pink nail-varnish.

Peter took new supplies from the container. Jaff slept in a typically exhausted fashion nearby and, leaning on the dog's broad back, Peter assembled his models. "I'm making two dinosaurs," he said. "Two fierce ones! They will have a big fight!"

Amelia looked up, grinning and caught sight of Ian's expression, which was thoughtful. For a moment, they held one another's gaze, before, abashed and faintly blushing, she bent to her sorting of building blocks again.

Heading for the kitchen, Robert said he was going to make a very large sandwich. His sister-in-law followed with the intention of supervising him; a fact he accepted placidly.

"Those building bricks were a good idea, of Ian's!" Margaret remarked. "They absorb Peter, when he gets tired of his drawings."

Robert agreed. "Yet, young Peter, is not needy, actually," he added. "He has put all his faith in his mother and she is extraordinary!"

"Have you noticed how well she gets along with Ian?" Margaret asked in her straightforward way, as she briskly sliced salad ingredients. "Did you see …?"

"Yes. Lately, I think they do get on well." He had spotted the exchange of glances. "I had thought … even, hoped …"

"Maria?"

"Mm." He was giving most of his attention to a cheese board, where there was a selection that included hard and soft cheeses of all kinds. After deliberating, he carefully cut a sizeable portion of blue cheese, spiked it on the end of a curved knife and added it to his plate, ignoring the raised brows of his sister–in-law. "They have often ridden out together and almost always come in laughing. He seems to pay attention …" He reflected for a moment and amended this. "Well, *some* attention to her words. I think in fact, she manages his behaviour very well!"

"Yes. Although, she really likes Elis!"

Robert accepted this. "We are in a situation where people will form bonds," he said. "Especially the young ones amongst us! For Ian, if it's going to be Amelia who can accept him for who he is, then my *reprehensible* grandson is very lucky. She is very talented, musical, and with many resources. If I permit myself a spot of self-interest, I must say, it is nice to see the child, Peter, around this old place, too."

Could Elis cope with a lively girl like Maria? Margaret allowed herself to wonder aloud, but Robert chuckled. "They are both very hard workers! But if you mean, in terms of having fun, I'd say he knows very well how to be humorous when he wants to!"

* * *

Ian was dressed casually for a ride. He said, he had no-one to do his washing. Maria barely let the remark touch her consciousness; she was certainly not going to offer to wash his riding breeches! However, her attention was caught when he put on gloves but insisted his hard hat was "lost somewhere". Instead, he had donned a tweed cap. It was a choice which made Maria frown. Most experienced riders can tell tales of people who thought they could ride so well they would never fall and hurt themselves, and many of those stories end in tears. The soft tweed cap was just like the one Elis wore, although it looked brand new. She wished Ian would wear a proper riding helmet. However, this was not up to her. Using the mounting block (like everyone who rode Cass), he got up on the horse and they set off.

Ian was an energetic rider and he urged his mount to canter often. Maria, herself a bold rider, easily kept up, riding Ed. When Ian rode Cass at a fallen tree, he leaned well forward as the horse made a huge leap and they cleared the trunk in fine style, but a hare leapt from tall grasses at the point where they landed. The startled horse threw up his head and leapt sideways, unseating Ian, who fell, landed heavily, and hit the back of his head on the ground.

"Oh God!" Ian lay on his back, holding his head with both hands. Maria dismounted and reached to take hold of the reins when Cass recovered from his fright and trotted back to them with an air of interest in his fallen rider. She watched Ian carefully, and although he lost all his colour, in a few moments he stood up. He even scrambled onto the tree trunk and mounted Cass again; nevertheless, he was very shaken. Quietly, they returned to the stables at a walk and Maria guessed that Ian was concentrating on staying upright. For the remainder of the ride, he was cautious, guiding Cass around any patches of long grass, keeping the pace very slow.

He spoke once more. "Ugh, I feel horrible … sorry Maria!"

In the stable yard, Maria dismounted first and held both horses, while Ian slid awkwardly from the saddle. He leaned against the wall of the tack room, while she led Ed and Cass into the stable block. As always, they pricked their ears and each made for the comfort of own stall. Working quickly, Maria loosened girths and secured stirrup irons. So that they could eat from their hay nets, she removed the horses' bridles and hung them temporarily on hooks nearby. After casting a glance at each water bucket, she returned to Ian, to walk beside him across the yard. He was squinting awkwardly because he was dazed, and Maria took his elbow to guide him. They went around the side of the house, mounted the two stone steps and entered via the porch as usual.

In the kitchen, Margaret was stirring something in a hot pan. She looked up as soon as she heard Maria's voice at the open doorway. Seeing Ian's shocked face, she hurried across the room with outstretched arms, while Maria described his fall, saying she thought he had hit his head quite hard. Ian made no argument, a fact which told both women he was feeling quite ill. Margaret knew what to do. Once he was seated in the easy chair, she began, gently, to examine his eyes and the back of his head.

Relieved, Maria left Ian in the capable hands of his aunt and returned to the yard to finish removing and tidying away the tack. She replaced the horses' daytime rugs, spoke to them calmly, secured their doors again, and then spent a few minutes attending to the parts of the tack that must be left clean. Once everything was in good order, she was able to leave the stables and begin to look after herself.

Later, after a shower and change of clothes, she rubbed her damp hair with a towel and plaited it. Downstairs, she found Amelia in the kitchen, making tea.

"Margaret says Ian can have a cup of tea now," Amelia said. "He doesn't seem to need a hospital dash. Oh, Maria!" She was emotional. Maria gave her a kind hug but their worries had eased and there was a general sense of relief.

When Amelia went away with her tray for Ian, at last Maria realised she, herself, was in need of a hot drink. She found a giant mug in the cupboard above the worktops, poured hot tea, added sugar and milk, then went to join Peter at the table. She reached for one of his chocolate biscuits.

"I'm going to read to Ian!" Peter was spreading story books over the tablecloth. "I might choose *Hey diddle-diddle ... the cow jumped over the moon!*"

"Well, it makes sense in a way!" Maria agreed.

"Mm," Peter tucked the book under his arm and climbed down from his chair. "Except, a *cow* isn't a *horse*," he laughed.

That night, Robert joined Margaret when she went to check on the invalid before she was ready to go to her own bedroom. When they left him for the night, Margaret returned to the sitting room to collect her book and a pair of spectacles, left on a chair arm. She observed to Robert that although Ian looked tired, he seemed comfortable.

"Hm ..." Robert was heading back to his fireside chair. "I had hoped such daredevil stunts were a thing of the past!"

Maria had decided to postpone her own further checks on Ian, considering his care was in the hands of the capable Margaret. She thought she would visit him after he had rested for a couple of days. She overhead Robert when, still addressing Margaret, he continued with an odd remark. "As a matter of fact, I can't count the number of times I've said the same thing in the past ... twice over, each time!"

* * *

Nigel paid a visit to the invalid during the next evening.

Ian had been asleep for most of the day but Margaret reported
that he ate his plate of poached fish, broccoli and creamed potatoes
with a good appetite. She was pleased, having planned the meal
carefully to be easily digestible.

If she had spotted her husband's behaviour later, she might have
been less satisfied with the state of Ian's digestion.

Passing the bedroom door as she went along the upper hallway,
Maria saw Nigel approach bearing a gleaming, embossed silver tray
with two crystal glasses and a small jug, generously filled with
brandy. He set this on a side table and put a forefinger to his lips,
then grasped the door handle and quietly turned it before reaching
to collect the tray. With a sidestep he entered the room

"For the shock," he murmured.

* * *

On the second morning after Ian's fall, Nigel unexpectedly offered
to ride with Maria. She was very pleased to have a companion. He
tacked up both horses while she prepared hay nets for their return.
He gave her a leg-up onto Ed before mounting Cass himself and
when they passed through gateways, he proved adept at opening the
metal catches with the tip of his riding crop.

There was no harm in Nigel. He was a large, hearty man with a
deep voice and energetic ways. He liked to ride at a good pace and
fortunately, Cass could carry his weight and even seemed, to Maria's
expert eye, to respond well to his rider.

Riding the smaller Ed, she cheerfully accompanied Nigel. He
had a better knowledge of the parkland and it was fun to keep up a
fast pace along tracks she had not discovered for herself. At last,
they let the horses walk on a loose rein, making their way down a
slight incline where a wide verge met a stony track. Maria let her
hips sway from side to side, accommodating Ed's downhill progress.
Nigel sat stolidly and it didn't matter; Cass easily bore his weight.
The horses stretched their necks, following the route they knew,

turning automatically to cross the track and head for the stable yard. Hooves squelched over mud and stones, then clattered as they arrived at the stable block.

"I enjoyed our ride!"

Maria had already kicked her feet out of the stirrup irons. She dismounted and unbuckled the straps of her riding cap.

"Yes, so did I, dear," answered Nigel equably, guiding Cass towards the mounting block, where he could dismount without difficulty. She couldn't help but contrast his easy company with the behaviour of the difficult Ian. Clearly, he respected the animals and after the ride he rubbed them down, collected their rugs, replenished water buckets and generally treated them well.

* * *

Elis came to call on Ian. Maria heard the arrival of a vehicle, and she was surprised when the farmer strode across the snow-covered gravel in front of the kitchen windows. There was a pause before he entered the great hallway.

"He'll be cleaning his boots!" remarked Margaret. Once inside the house, he greeted the ladies briefly with a raised hand when he passed by the open kitchen door. He had every appearance of composure, almost, thought Maria, like someone who was well-used to the house. He folded his cap and stuffed it into his jacket pocket, before making his way up the carpeted staircase to Ian's bedroom, where he stayed for an hour, chatting quietly.

No laughter could be heard from the men but all seemed peaceful, although, when he returned downstairs, Elis' dark hair stood on end, looking as if he had been running his hands through it. Again, he turned his head and briefly waved to acknowledge Margaret and Maria.

Maria was not absolutely sure what her thoughts were at that moment but when he paused to pull on his ancient tweed cap, he gave her a grin through the depths of his beard and something seemed to be making its way to the forefront of her mind. She wanted to ask him to stay, to show him that she would welcome his company but found herself unusually shy. As she struggled with this emotion, she found herself taking a step forward but it was too late. Elis collected his greatcoat from the tiled floor of the anteroom, shrugged into it, and swiftly left.

Peter appeared in the sitting room with a message. Ian had eaten his sandwiches. Please could he have cake? The child immediately ran off, explaining his haste with an over-the-shoulder comment. "I'm reading to him!"

In Ian's room, Maria found him sitting up in bed with pillows behind his shoulders. He was drinking coffee. A crust and a fragment of cold ham were all that remained on a plate on his lap, and he appeared alert and cheerful despite looking wan in the face. He had an impressive black eye. "Hey," he said, when he saw Maria enter the room. "I'm better!"

Margaret bent down to pick up a fallen blanket. She tucked it neatly over the lower end of his bed. "Well, you're getting there! Might do quite well if you keep eating and drinking at this rate." She tweaked the blanket until it was very smooth.

"I'm all tucked in tightly," he grumbled, trying to move his feet.

Amelia was seated beside the invalid and Peter stood at her knee, holding a spilling armful of story books. With a hand on Amelia's shoulder, Maria reached behind her to place the cake in its serviette on a bedside table.

"How on earth did he get a swollen *eye?*" She stood back to observe Ian. "Ugh, it makes me feel sick!" She didn't want him to think she was especially sympathetic.

"It's just where the swelling went," said Margaret, placidly, giving the bedcovers a final firm pat.

Ian made a vulgar gesture towards Maria, cupping his hand with the other in deference to Peter's presence. "Can't frown," he mentioned. He rearranged pillows behind his head. "Or smile."

There was bruising on his cheek too. Maria hated it but she made herself sound casual.

"No, so it seems!" she answered him.

"I suppose he was thrown down so hard …" Margaret was following a train of thought, but she stopped when Amelia drew in a sharp breath. "Don't think about it!" she advised, instead.

"I really can't!" Amelia shook her head. "We should probably leave you in peace," she told Ian. "C'mon Peter!" She helped to gather up the books, and took her son by the hand.

"I'll read again, tomorrow!" Peter assured Ian, who was leaning back into his pillows now.

"See you then," he murmured.

Margaret turned a dimmer switch on the wall, making the bedroom light very low. Then she collected Ian's empty coffee cup and the discarded plate before she, too, left the room.

"Maria," Ian's voice stayed her when she would have followed Margaret at once. "Thanks for getting me home. That was … I was …" He was looking at Maria but, for once, he seemed lost for words. Was he feeling emotional?

"Don't think about it!" Firmly, Maria echoed Margaret's instruction to Amelia. Yet, she stood still, regarding the pale, bruised face in the pillows. Without his disarming grin, his familiar appearance was different and yet his expression seemed to strike a chord within her. He was more lovable, somehow. It wasn't a thought she welcomed; nevertheless, she found herself speaking kindly. "Poor you!"

Maria hadn't wanted to reveal how anxious she had felt about him since the fall. Suddenly, her guard was slipping. He heard the compassion in her voice, and reached out for her. Time seemed to stand still in the darkened room, while she hesitated, then took his hand and held it briefly. She looked down at his long fingers with their fine manicure. When she glanced up and saw his serious gaze, she recovered her composure. She would not let herself fall into those dark eyes. Instead, she withdrew. "Sleep well," she told him, then turned away and quietly left without looking back.

* * *

The afternoon was peaceful, for Maria. Ian, not so well recovered as he pretended, was sleeping. Amelia and Margaret set off for the village shop, taking Peter, both for something to do and to fetch a few groceries. Maria wished them well but she had no interest in paying a visit to the hostile pair, Sue and Jackie.

In the house, where Robert had taken himself upstairs to nap and both dogs were absent having followed Nigel who went on foot on an expedition to a neighbouring farm, she was by herself.

Maria felt faintly unreal at first and the contrast between being amongst a group of chattering people and wandering about in the silence that now fell, seemed vast. Deliberately, she shook off her sense of loneliness and went to check the fire in the sitting-room, where she knelt to add small pieces of wood, then a heavy log to top it up.

Now, with no voices to disturb the peace, she heard the background sounds of the house: the crackle of flames in dry wood, the clicks and whirrs made by the gas central-heating. She curled herself into the corner of a deep sofa and thought about Amelia.

When Amelia arrived at the mansion, a waif rescued from the storm, she looked barely more than a child herself. Now, she bloomed. Her cheeks were pink with the complexion of the classic English rose; her eyes shone and her pretty fair hair was allowed to wave around the sweet oval of her face. She carried herself with new dignity.

Maria was glad she had persuaded the girl to trim and free up her curly hair, and since then they had shared make-up and perfume too. She knew Robert with his gentle and immaculate manners had helped to restore self-esteem for Amelia, while Margaret had willingly given her flattering sweaters, as well as a good deal of kindly mothering.

Where did that sparkle come from? Maria suspected it was because of Ian. She thought about the way Amelia couldn't bear to think about his fall. She was sensitive about him. Would he return the compliment and see Amelia for the valuable person she really was?

* * *

Margaret wasn't one to panic and Ian was not a child. Nevertheless, it seemed a call to his parents could be in order. He was on the mend for sure, but they had a right to know about an event which was quite shocking. Maria wondered, in a fleeting thought, whether he would agree to this. Would he be difficult? Instead, he chose to be agreeable. He was in accord with Margaret. However, he was keen to let them know what had happened without causing undue worry.

"Auntie Marg' it's okay, I'll call them myself! Then mother will find out but she won't have time to feel scared because I can tell her I'm doing well!"

It was a thoughtful plan, and after Ian had eaten breakfast, he put it into action. He requested the landline to be brought and plugged in beside his bed, saying his damned mobile would probably keep cutting out. He placed the call, sitting up amongst pillows, still very sore but looking better. Maria found him talking fairly animatedly when she popped upstairs to collect his breakfast tray.

"So, I feel much better!" he was saying, with the telephone receiver held to his ear. Seeing Maria come to his side, he spoke to her abstractedly. "Thanks, darling!"

Maria tidied the bedside table and carefully stacked and gathered together crockery, cutlery, miniature jam and marmalade pots, and leftover toast crusts. Then, lifting the tray, she straightened and began to cross the carpet towards the doorway. She walked with a typically erect back, but stiffly. Ian finished his conversation with his mother just as she neared the end of his bed. He called her.

"Maria!"

She paused and half-turned but she kept her eyes on the items she had gathered up.

He knew. "I shouldn't have said *thanks darling*!"

Maria was frank, as always. "No." She looked up. "It sounded like ... either, I was a maid or a wife!"

He could smile today. "Both those things?"

"Said nicely, I suppose it's a term of endearment ..."

"Term of endearment then?" he asked. "Alright?"

"Well ..."

"Oh Maria." Ian looked a little nonplussed. He had replaced the telephone on its receiver at the bedside. Lying back with his hands loosely in his lap, he seemed tired again, and somewhat vulnerable. "I don't think ... I honestly don't think, by now, that I can't say something nice to you. I mean, why not?"

She took pity on him and spoke more gently before she left the room. "I'm glad you feel better, and you can smile now!"

"Thanks!"

At the threshold, she hesitated. "With a numb face, I guess you can't wink? Good thing!" She left, managing the tray on one arm for a moment while she closed the door behind her. She heard a pillow hit the other side, with a thump.

Robert's Story

As the days flowed by, the occupants of the old mansion felt at ease with one another. They had shared stories, laughter and compassionate times and there was a real sense of familiarity with one another as Christmas Day approached.

Robert became expansive at last, and he told them something of his personal story.

"I went to school with Sarah. We were best friends as children, and she waited for me at the crossroads at the top of the village every morning, and in primary school she always sat beside me. We shared many happy days as children, and married when we were both twenty-two years of age. But even so, the year before we were wed, I fell in love with a gypsy girl!"

"Robert!" exclaimed Margaret. "*Really?*"

The revelation wasn't new, to Nigel. "He did. I remember how angry and worried our father was. I was only about eight. I saw the horse-drawn caravans in the town, and I knew where they made their camp. I hung around, until someone who knew my dad spotted me, but one of the men had already given me a lurcher puppy. I was allowed to keep him, our parents liked working dogs." He fell silent, the flow of memories halted at the point of the long-ago puppy. Then he mentioned, "Robert's gypsy girl had long, tangled, black hair."

"… and a hand-span waist. She could really dance," said Robert. He sighed. "Ah me. But it was not to be and of course, I had many joyful years with my dear wife. There are many ways to fall in love."

There was a silence while his companions digested this. Ian was frowning.

"What was her name, Robert?" Margaret asked.

Robert and Nigel both spoke together, but when the latter said "Jo", Robert said "Rose!" The pair did not argue. Mystified, their listeners were silent again.

"*A rose,*" quoted Robert reflectively, "*by any other name, would smell as sweet!*"

At length, Ian spoke. "Quite an adventure, granddad! Was it painful or wonderful?"

"It was painful then. Now, it is a treasured memory."

* * *

After Robert's revelations, Margaret seemed to feel in need of something to distract her. She made herself a cup of tea, before delving into her handbag to find a daisy-patterned notebook and a slim, silver pen. These items, she carried upstairs to place on the writing desk in her bedroom. Fortified by tea, she sat there and carefully planned her order of work in readiness for Christmas Day.

A small sound behind Margaret made her start. Turning around, she saw Peter, who had followed her upstairs. He was awake a little later than usual, although he was wearing the oversized shirt which served as his sleeping attire. She was thankful that he was so young; he couldn't have grasped all the implications there were in Robert's story. Sure enough, he asked no questions; instead, impressed by her notetaking, he asked her for a sheet of paper and said he would make notes, too. She supplied him with a few pages of her lined paper, found a second pen in her handbag, and shared her table top with him. Before she recommended her own lists, prudently she went across the room and set the door ajar, so that Amelia would find Peter easily once she was ready to put him to bed.

Peter was very pleased. He discussed the dinner ahead in a grown-up way and made a number of important squiggles on the pages, leaning on a cardboard storybook about Black Beauty. He wrote his name correctly a few times, and drew a picture of a giant Christmas cracker.

Amelia knew Peter's whereabouts. Relieved of her responsibilities for a while, she decided to let her small son enjoy an extra thirty minutes before his bedtime. She collected a couple of empty glasses and followed Maria, who was on her way into the kitchen to feed the dogs. She bent to stroke the patient Jaff when he got to his feet with his eye on Maria's activities, and turned to open the door again for Boy, who had been lying at Robert's feet but could now be heard scrabbling urgently from the other side.

Maria opened a tin, filled dishes with meaty food and placed them on the tiled floor, jumping aside with an exclamation as Boy barged in and almost knocked her over. She washed her hands then took a clean white tea-towel from a drawer to dry them and turned back to the sink to wipe some draining crockery. She was aware that Amelia's manner was diffident when she spoke, to ask, would Maria like a cup of tea?

Maria accepted and leaned against the sink, facing Amelia, waiting. The younger woman plunged into her question with an air of desperation, as she began to assemble teacups and saucers. "Maria, about Ian ... you were here ahead of me. You get on well with him, don't you?"

Maria didn't answer the question straight away. "We'll get tea," she declared, crossing the room to help Amelia, who was pouring milk with a shaking hand. She took the jug and gave her a comforting pat on the shoulder. "Then we'll take our tray upstairs," she went on. "We can sit on my bed and talk."

They covered themselves with a thick blanket and lay together, facing one another. There was not, after all, so much to say. Maria confessed she was besotted with Elis. "Oh Amelia! I can't explain what has happened! Yet he is so serious. How is he serious and still fascinating?"

They smiled at each other.

"This could work out very well, if Elis …" Amelia broke off. She looked thoughtful. "See if you *can* make him lighten up! Try!"

"I have seen him grin …" dubiously, Maria answered. "It's just not his usual way. It's an awkward thing though, because I wouldn't want to change him."

"I know." Amelia ploughed through her defences. "But this is the rest of your life you're planning, with a very solemn soul. I've seen how you laugh with Ian. I know you love to have fun! Take care, Maria."

Her bravery was amazing, Maria thought. Amelia herself was becoming fond of Ian, so it was daring for her to suggest that her friend might compare the two men. "I'll tell you how I know it's Elis, for me," she said. "He doesn't actually say very much. He hasn't spent much time with me. Nothing, or not much, has happened between him and me but he seems to read my mind. There's just … there's simply …" She broke off and found, to her dismay, she was becoming tearful.

Amelia put her small hands on each side of Maria's face. "Tell me what you mean?"

"Surely, all these feelings must mean that I've fallen in love with him?"

* * *

Robert was very conscious that his household, which included some people who should have considered themselves only welcome guests, was very busy.

One morning, just a couple of days before Christmas Day, he entered the great lounge, where the welcome crackle of a freshly stoked fire could be heard. Lamps still glowed in the dim light, while the heavy drapes remained closed against the early chill.

Dressed in a silk dressing gown over his daytime shirt and trousers, Robert lifted aside a curtain and stood at the window to look at the parkland outside. The grounds were snow-covered by this time, although not deeply. There were patches of icy snow around the edges of the courtyard immediately in front of the tall windows, and a low wall was white-topped. Across the park, a few deer ran into woodland and disappeared into the darkness of the trees.

Robert made a decision. They could drive out, in the Range Rover. He turned and went into the kitchen, where Margaret and Nigel were eating toast and marmalade and drinking tea. Amelia and Maria had begun to cook bacon, in readiness for the larger breakfasts favoured by Robert himself, and Ian. The friendly atmosphere was comforting to the old man, who spent so much of his time alone during the year. He announced his intention to treat everyone to lunch at the pub. They would be a party of seven; he would call to reserve a table.

"A pub that takes reservations?" Maria was unused to such a thing.

"For Robert, they do!" Ian told her.

Margaret demurred at first, saying she was busy.

"Busy?" asked Robert. "*Busy?* So are the ants! Question is, what are you *busy about?*"

Peter got her round the waist in a hug and her mind was changed, especially when Nigel remembered the pub served "good puddings".

"Let's dress up and look smart," she said then, to Maria and Amelia.

* * *

When Margaret emerged from her room, she sported a large hat made of pale faux fur, and a long camel coat. At her neck, tucked in neatly, was a silky scarf in a brilliant shade of royal blue. Pulling on a pair of soft leather gloves, she joined the others.

Nigel kissed her cheek. "You look just like Britt Ekland," he said, gallantly.

Then Maria arrived at the foot of the stairs. She too wore a long coat, buttoned smartly. She had brushed her hair and left it loose; hanging behind her shoulders it fell in a glossy curtain to her waist. She caught sight of her reflection in a long mirror, and paused to adjust the collar of her blouse. The coat was dark grey and it was fitted, with a narrow belt. Ian was admiring. "You look lovely in that coat!"

"Thanks!" She acknowledged the compliment but, making herself deliberately casual, she turned away from his gaze to hold out her hand to Peter. From the corner of her eye, she saw Ian looked rueful before he transferred his attention to Amelia, who had followed her down the staircase, walking carefully since she wore a pair of Margaret's high-heeled boots. He stepped forward to offer a courteous helping hand when she reached the bottom step, smiled down at her once she stood beside him, and took the furry jacket she had slung over her arm, to help her put it on.

They enjoyed a delicious lunch of hot pies and vegetables, served steaming and buttered. There were jugs full of rich gravy and a selection of sauces. Ian was careful to drink just one small lager, then later drove the Range Rover steadily home, where he fortified himself with a generous glass of red wine and proposed a game of Monopoly.

Robert declined and settled himself in his armchair near the fire, where he read a newspaper for a while before declaring with dignity he would take "a short post prandial …" He fell into a doze. Margaret, saying she couldn't concentrate on a game, went off to make coffee for them all. Peter shared his place on the board with his mother until he fell asleep on Nigel's lap and was transferred to the sofa. Maria gave the game her best shot but seemed to be unlucky;

at last, she excused herself and went to put on her jeans and jacket, so that she could brave the cold air outside to look after the horses and dogs.

Nigel was competitive and turned back to the board after settling Peter but he was not the winner. He retired with good grace eventually and Ian (who soundly beat everyone in the game) sat on with Amelia at the table where they drank coffee, chatting and laughing together.

Later, Amelia hurried to the foot of the staircase, where she remembered leaving some of her belongings hanging on the balustrade. Something had diverted her attention after the group returned from their lunchtime outing. In this lovely mansion, as a rule, no-one left their possessions lying about. She was relieved to see Ian's greatcoat had also been left casually nearby, draped over the back of an oak bench. Amelia slipped her silk scarf around her neck, slung her handbag over her shoulder and looked down, fastening a buckle.

"Amelia!" Ian had followed her from the lounge; he put his hand on her shoulder and gently turned her to face him. "Amelia, can we talk again?"

She looked up, not shy as she had been at the start of her stay but positively sparkling with joy and confidence. Her expression told him she would talk again. Coming back indoors after the cold trip to the stables, where the horses were resting that afternoon, Maria glanced towards the lower staircase when she heard voices. She could tell, this was not a moment to intrude.

ANOTHER VISIT

When Elis arrived and asked for Robert, Maria did not know why he called again but it was, after all, not her business. She saw him as he made his way over the gravel and overheard his comments as he arrived at the door and spoke to Margaret to enquire after Robert's health and whether he might pay him a visit.

Jess and Seb' were ordered to wait in the back porch while their master went to find Robert in the study. With impressive obedience, they settled themselves beneath a row of heavy coats, where they curled up amongst a collection of wellington boots and fallen scarves. Maria was on her way to the stables to care for the horses in the final visit of the day, but she tore herself away from the house reluctantly. She took a handful of gravy biscuits for the dogs, wondering if Elis would still be there, when she returned.

In this, she was not disappointed. Elis was seated by the great hearth, drinking pale sherry, chatting with Nigel. When the family offered a hot supper, he politely declined, but Margaret would not be thwarted of every appearance of a hospitable welcome and she filled a plate with cold beef sandwiches for the two men and persuaded Maria to take it to them. Maria felt self-conscious there in the luxurious room, since she still wore her riding breeches. The conversation was mainly about sheep and she had little to offer.

Elis left before long, with a courteous "goodbye" to everyone before he went out of the back door with his dogs hastening to his side from their spot beneath the coats.

Maria stood at the window and watched him leave. She saw him pull his cap down over his forehead as he trudged through a heavy snowfall. Disconsolate and unable to hide it, she let her shoulders slump. Margaret noticed her demeanour but Amelia, who was engaged in whisking batter for a pudding, did not.

"He's a cool customer!" Amelia remarked, with relative disinterest.

When the door slammed behind Elis, Maria was disappointed. His figure looked lonely, marching away. She sighed, feeling deprived of a proper chat. *"Why did he come?"* she wondered aloud. *"Why wouldn't he stay?"*

"I know," said Margaret unexpectedly. "He visited to talk about the flock because they're getting more sheep, plus there'll be lambing soon and he needs to take on a helper. He wasn't really rushing off, as such. I mean, he's always the same, staying just for the time it takes to sort things out for the farm. Robert talked to him first, then went upstairs to change for dinner. When you came in from the stables, Elis was still speaking with Nigel. He very rarely stays here for long enough to relax ... *oh!*" She had dropped an iron pan with a great crash. She stopped speaking abruptly, bent to pick it up, and took it to the sink, to wipe it in case it had picked up dog hair.

"The sheep are Robert's?" That made sense. "But, why would Elis decline to spend more time here, for dinner and a chat?" Maria's voice sounded disgruntled, even to her own ears! For a moment, the three women were silent but in response to a call from her son, Amelia left the room and Margaret continued with her train of thought.

"Maria, he watches you. It was the first time I've seen that, but I think it's true. When I came into the sitting room to collect the sandwich plates, I noticed he was still talking about the great barn and the pens for the new lambs, but his eyes were on you. You were staring at the fire. But he lives in that tiny cottage. Here, it's ... well ... grand, isn't it? Very comfortable. Then, when the snow has gone, Robert will have his usual groom and cook back but you're an independent woman and you will leave, probably ... although ..."

Her voice tailed off, she was trying to get her words right, but Maria guessed what she would have said, if it hadn't been such a sensitive thought. "Ian?"

"I mean, I don't know for sure ... and I can't read minds! Still, I'd say, there could seem to be certain choices ahead for you. Elis might feel he shouldn't get involved or try to alter anything you decide. Do you see?"

Maria sighed and stood back from the cold glass, then turned around with a solemn expression. Margaret was quiet for a moment, crumbling gravy cubes into one of her pans. She glanced at Maria's face. "Don't be offended!"

"Of course not!" Maria accepted all this. "I'm not offended at all, although I think there is something to put right, here. Surely, I need to let him know I'm not staying with Ian?"

"Yes!" Margaret agreed. "If that's the case, I think perhaps you do!" She was privately relieved, since she was acutely aware of the growing interest between Ian and Amelia. They were spending time together. In her motherly way, Margaret felt it was good for Ian to stop flirting pointlessly with the self-possessed Maria and learn how to be courtly. A sudden roar from outside could be heard as the wind strengthened. Firmly, she added, "there is nothing to be done, for the moment!"

They closed the kitchen curtains, blotting out the dark sky and whirling snowflakes; then went around the house doing the same in the sitting room, the dining room and the main study. In upper hallways, blinds and drapes were drawn over the narrower windows too. Margaret turned on lamps and held a match to three giant white candles that stood in a row within the great hearth, where a bright fire burned, replenished with logs brought in by Nigel and Ian.

Before long, they went back to the kitchen and their cookery.

* * *

Amelia entered the room, and returned to her batter. She peered into the bowl. "It's bubbly!" Margaret said it didn't matter, batter always improved with standing. Amelia picked up her wooden spoon. She remembered their conversation.

"Do you think Elis was worried about getting up the hill to his cottage, in the snow and storm?" she asked. "Is that why he wouldn't eat with us?" Her back was turned towards the other women.

Maria glanced at Margaret, who shook her head. It would be a shame if, like Elis, Amelia imagined no one must come between Ian and Maria when they were not destined to be together in any case. Even if they discussed what Elis might be thinking and explained he was wrong, the very thought of Ian being interested in Maria in any realistic way could be painful for Amelia, and needlessly upsetting. Privately, Maria reflected that this was true, even though she and Amelia had spoken together about her feelings for Elis.

So, since she had phrased her question in a convenient way, it was perfectly possible to reply simply. "Well, it's possible!" Margaret agreed. "Yes, perhaps he was worried about the storm."

* * *

After Elis declined dinner on that snowy night, Maria began to see his behaviour as truly challenging. Could Elis have thought that once she was in the Manse and living as part of Robert's household, she would find Ian irresistible? It was only guesswork she supposed, but there was a strong possibility that Margaret was correct and Elis had drawn certain conclusions. The idea made her feel annoyed! Maria had a mind of her own.

She shared the fireside with Margaret and Amelia. Peter was asleep and the men were playing cards in the study. They were doings things properly, as Robert explained with satisfaction, with cigars (even though none of them smoked as a rule), whisky in tumblers beside their elbows, and a competitive attitude that meant they were gambling for cash! They were best left to it, Margaret thought. She had a recipe book on her knee and a steaming cup of tea at her elbow.

Amelia's mind was on romance. "D'you think Robert could have loved the gypsy girl and his wife *equally? Can* a man love two women?"

"The French think so," Maria replied.

"Was she beautiful, I wonder?" Her companions guessed she referred to Rose.

"She had very curly black hair and a tiny waist and feet!" supplied Margaret. The others looked at her in surprise; she was much younger than Robert. "Nigel remembers," she said. "He told me a bit more about those times."

"Ah," Amelia was still entranced by the story. "Was *Sarah b*eautiful?" she asked, hoping so. Maria nodded, having seen the pictures in Robert's room.

"Delicate and fair," Margaret told Amelia. "She was very similar to you, as a matter of fact!"

Maria remembered Robert chose to call the girl Rose even though her name was Jo, according to his brother. She considered his reflective quote, when she admired the picture of his wedding toast ... *days of wine and roses.* 'I think he recalls them both lovingly," she said. "Respectfully, too. They were of equal charm to him, I'm sure of it."

On the subject of respect, the women began to discuss Ian. Amelia was quick to say, she thought being funny was not the same as being too cheeky and her companions smiled at that. There was a pause.

"Elis can be funny too," reflected Maria. She told the other women about the incident with the shrew, describing the way Elis teased her for hanging on to her manners despite her shock.

"Swear words let you down!" Margaret approved of her self-restraint. "Even though he laughed, I expect he liked you all the better for it."

"I'll get him!" declared Maria. "I'll get him by …" She broke off and gazed at nothing in particular.

Amelia chuckled. The penny dropped a moment later for Margaret, who exclaimed aloud. *"Maria!"*

"He might think you're just a tart!" Amelia warned, bluntly.

With composure, Maria answered "Robert didn't think Gypsy Rose was a tart! She is still a treasured memory."

"Yeah …" Amelia considered this. "That's kind of the point! If you turn into a memory, it means you were left behind. You should want more than that, too!"

"So far as I know, Elis has no one else in mind." Margaret was recovering from the revelations from Maria but she decided a second cup of tea might restore her further. Rising from her chair, she continued her train of thought. "It's a different situation, because Robert was always going to marry Sarah." She became blunt, herself. "You should probably go for it!"

"Go for what?" Nigel entered the sitting room carrying a bundle of magazines and newspapers as well as an open box of chocolates. "Who should?" He headed for the sofa, placed reading material and treats on a nearby coffee table and contentedly began to make a cosy nest of some cushions and a throw. In an aside, he went on. "Thrashed, and the poorer for it!"

"Nothing, dear!" Margaret was airy. She seemed suspiciously well-practised in evident innocence, but the younger ladies giggled and raided his chocolate box before they all left him on his own.

CHRISTMAS

Peter fell asleep after lunch, having a short day as children often do after all the excitement on Christmas morning.

Outside the mansion the wind blew strongly, howling eerily around the rooftop. Everyone was cosy inside but Maria, with a thick sweater underneath her jacket, had to battle her way across the yard to the stables with the gusts of cold air making her catch her breath as she ran. Inside their stalls, Ed and Cass were pleased to see Maria as always, but their behaviour was placid. Supplied with food and fresh water as well as armfuls of clean straw, they were all set to rest quietly and did not appear to be expecting to go out. Perhaps they recognised the shrieking of the wind as a sign they were best inside.

Maria chatted to the horses as she tidied the stalls and filled hay nets but when she stooped to collect an empty bucket, she got a push from Ed's long nose which nearly overbalanced her. "Fine!" she said to him. "I'm going!"

When, thankfully, she re-entered the porch, the contrast between the outside world and the peaceful interior of the house was immediate. Her skin was damp with icy raindrops and strands of hair clung to her cheeks. She found a towel in the small washroom off the porch and utility area and went into the kitchen, rubbing at her face to dry it. As the storm continued to rage, the occupants of the old mansion marvelled at the strength of the wind and told one another they were glad to be safely indoors. After all, relaxed and full of good humour, they enjoyed luxurious comfort in that lovely place.

At bedtime, Maria made her way along the dimly-lit upper hall to enter her suite, where the warmth of a long radiator made it snug. Twice more, she had forced herself to go outside to check on the horses and she spent some time in the stables, settling them for the night. Now she closed her door with a sense of relief, before crossing the room, which was not in complete darkness thanks to the golden glow of a low light set inside an agate stone. She drew long, blue velvet curtains over the window. Just before pulling them fully together, she paused, staring through the glass towards darkened parkland and lawns faintly illuminated by outdoor lights, realising there was a silence because the wind had dropped.

It would snow again, Maria felt sure. The air was so very cold. After covering the icy-cold window, she moved cautiously in the darkness, to switch on a bedside lamp. In its soft glow, she turned down her cream cotton sheets and shook up the plump white quilt on the bed. She made a pile of pillows, then slid under the covers, to lean comfortably and write in her diary. Maria recorded only the events of her day; she did not confide her most private thoughts to the pages of her journal but as she fell asleep, she thought about Elis, whose dark gaze lingered in her memory.

* * *

The following morning Maria awoke to a room still in shadows. She fished for her mobile phone beneath her pillows and saw the time was just six o'clock. Dawn would not come yet on this wintry day.

It was Boxing Day and the household would no doubt be peaceful; people might even sleep later than usual, into the morning. There were no sounds other than the soft, background hum of the central heating system.

A fringed shawl lay folded beside Maria, and she wrapped it around her shoulders, got out of bed and, holding her phone for its light, padded barefoot over the thick, caramel-coloured carpet to peer between the drapes at the world outside.

Snow blanketed the world, lying thickly over every surface, pure-white and icy-cold.

* * *

"Christmas is great!" Nigel declared on Boxing Day. He wore a red, paper hat, which he had pulled down over his forehead to ensure it wouldn't slip off his head. He was assembling slices of cold meat on his plate. "Good leftovers in the cold cabinets; a massive fire in the hearth and champagne on the drinks table!"

"Nigel!" His wife was reproving. "Get some salad to go beside that meat!"

He wouldn't. He added a generous spoonful of pickle and observed that it was enough. It was an elegant sufficiency, consider-ing it was only his brunch.

"I worry about his heart," Margaret confessed honestly, after her husband had left the room.

Maria tried to think of something positive to say. She mentioned that the ride she and Nigel shared on Cass and Ed was not only great fun but really seemed to show he was very strong. "Thank you for that!" Margaret was grateful. "Yes, he's always energetic and of course he's naturally a big man. I suppose it's just that he is so important to me …"

Ian was making a sandwich of his own, quietly putting in the same tasty ingredients as Nigel. He spooned pickle over ham and flattened a doorstep of bread on top. "Nigel's a lucky man, Auntie Margaret," he told her. "It must be very nice to have someone to worry about you, and who wants to look after you!"

A main meal later in the day consisted of more slices of cold turkey and ham, generously heaped on a giant platter surrounded by dishes of pickles, salad, baked potatoes and buttered Brussels sprouts. As always, one or two people at the table thought that the Boxing Day meal was often even nicer than Christmas Dinner. The television was switched on so that old films could be watched or, in the case of Robert and Nigel who were comfortably ensconced in armchairs, to create a background sound for their naps.

* * *

After Boxing Day, which fell on a Monday, a prospective shepherd's boy arrived from the village, to begin a new job. With lambing ahead, there would be work for him at the croft. Ian was absent and Nigel had accompanied him on his round of the farms. Robert, a little diffident, asked Maria if she would show the young man the route. Since she was, after all, in Robert's employment and in fact had no objection, she went ahead and, after taking care to dress herself in a thick jacket, mittens and a scarf, she led the way uphill.

Elis was there, standing in the open doorway with his hands in the pockets of a heavy sheepskin jacket. Its collar was turned up around his bearded face, and his tweed cap was pulled low on his brow.

"Hello."

Maria couldn't read his expression but she had been sent by Robert, after all. She indicated, to her right, the young man, who had lingered near the yard instead of following Maria directly and was looking at the fields behind the croft.

"I was asked to bring the new shepherd!" She sounded faintly defensive, and half-expected to see a gleam of amusement in the fathomless dark eyes, but his gaze remained direct and steady and he seemed to be waiting for more. With that awareness, she wouldn't be disingenuous. "I wanted to come back!" Taking a small risk, she told him this. "I said I was happy to bring the shepherd!"

Maria spent a comfortable hour, cuddling Smoke and resting by the fireside while Elis took the new employee to see the sheep. By the time he returned he had shed his companion, since their business was arranged and the young man had set off on his way back to the village by himself.

Maria was sleepy. She sat up with flushed cheeks when she heard the door swing open, and the heavy panting of the dogs as they rushed in. Jaws already dripping from their outdoor water bowl, they greeted her, pushing against her hands, demanding pats.

"Ugh!"

She pressed her fingers against her jeans to dry them. She hoped the lad would not get lost; she had stayed because she meant to guide him back. Elis said he had people coming, he was getting five new sheep of a different type from the others,

Maria felt she should go. However, he seemed keen to show her the preparations for the new lambs. Tempted by this because of her love of animal care, shaking off sleep, she got her jacket from one of the hooks on the wall and was ready to follow him out into the cold air again.

The barn was full of the scent of new straw, with bales stacked to create separate pens for each lambing ewe, when they were ready. Water troughs were plentiful, small halters and ropes hung against the walls; covered tubs were full of foodstuffs for the animals. Maria felt privileged to see all this.

They left the barn, with Elis turning to lock the wide doors carefully. Watching him, Maria stepped backwards, somehow, into a patch of boggy ground and was revolted when cold, muddy water splashed and soaked her feet. "I should go," she decided. "I shan't want to take these off and then put them on again straight away!"

Elis seemed reluctant to let her leave. "Stay," he suggested. "We can get a drink. I will put your shoes by the fire."

In the house, he knelt to help her remove the wet boots and bore them off, along with her damp socks, to place in the hearth. Their rain-soaked coats were slung across the backs of kitchen chairs. When he straightened and turned to pull the two easy chairs near the warmth of the fire, Maria felt self-conscious but now there was no denying they were both aware of a closeness. They faced each other and it was an uncertain moment for Maria. *There are people coming,* she reminded herself privately.

"When we spoke before, you said it was lovely at the big house ..." Elis bent to unlace his own boots and after kicking them off on the doormat, he went to take tumblers and a small bottle of whisky from a wall cupboard. Maria hesitated before answering his comment, which seemed to be both a statement and a question.

In the pause, he offered a drink. She refused the alcohol, since she had yet to attend to the horses' evening care but asked if she could make a cup of coffee. He left the glasses on the counter, switched the kettle on for her and went to sit in his chair, diverted as he waited for her response to his interest in her life at the Manse. Maria wondered if this was more than a mild interest.

"I did say it was lovely," she agreed. She hesitated before going on, intending to explain her thoughts, wanting to avoid a misunderstanding. "I didn't mean, because of the beautiful things ... the wealth, you know." She risked a comment. "It's also lovely *here.*"

Elis was listening intently and she expanded on this. "What matters to me, is, feeling welcome ... feeling warmth. Also, caring about animals and getting things just right for them." She might have added, *good company.* She didn't want to look too obvious.

Elis pulled Smoke from behind him and settled himself; leaning back in his chair, he stretched his legs then absently rubbed Jess on her stomach with the toes of his right foot.

Maria poured whisky into a single glass and handed it to Elis, then made her hot drink and sat on the hearthrug. She would have loved to lean against the rough material of his trousers. Instead, she sat upright, watching the flames in the fireplace. Elis seemed thoughtful, and they both fell silent. A clock's steady tick could be heard. In a little while, he sighed and leaned forward. Without warning he abandoned his typical reserve, to brush a lock of hair from her cheek. A little startled, Maria looked at him, keeping very still, holding her breath. He copied her own familiar gesture, to draw her long plait over her shoulder. He ran fingertips over her brow, and again a second time, as if to smooth away a frown. He brushed her lips with his thumb, tracing the surrounding freckles. He did these things very slowly. He was teasing her.

Marisa drew a breath, at last. "Hey!" She caught his long fingers in her hands but she kept them pressed against her throat.

"Talk to me, Maria! You're such a lively person! Are you sure of those thoughts? Is it enough for you, to be here?"

His unexpected touches were fractionally cheeky. Also, seductive. When he seemed to linger on her lips, he stirred her and now she regarded him with glowing eyes … but despite the sweet temptation of his teasing, his expression remained fairly serious. Was there a smile playing around the corners of his mouth? It was hard to tell, but his next words revealed the depth of his meaning. "Here … with me?"

Maria remained very still but her thoughts were full of questions. Their body language was changing fast now. Still, she wondered. How did Elis know she was so close to wanting to stay with him for ever?

There was a knock at the door, the dogs barked and their intimate moment was interrupted. Elis got up to answer the caller. He found, not his couple of expected visitors but Nigel, who wore a riding helmet and carried another.

"Maria, I've brought the horses. There's going to be a big storm; the rain has started and already washed away most of the snow on the track. Margaret was worrying about you. I'll see you safely back, if you want to come with me now!" His words were well-meant. Her trip up to the croft was, after all, the result of being asked by Robert to bring the shepherd as a special favour.

Nevertheless, Nigel's arrival was a dreadful intrusion! Apparently oblivious to this, he bent and patted the dogs as they greeted him with wagging tails. Maria, standing now, finished her coffee and set the mug on the counter before pulling on her jacket. The wet socks she stuffed into a pocket before stooping to push her feet uncomfortably into her still-soaked boots. Straightening, she saw Elis take a swallow of his whisky and saw, too, he had a face like thunder. She could not catch his eye and there was no opportunity to reassure him, so she rammed the hat on her head and left the croft with Nigel. A gust of wind caught the door, which closed with a bang.

With a leg-up from Nigel, Maria was up and into Ed's saddle in a moment. Her walking boots were too broad for the stirrups, so she crossed the leathers and irons in front of the saddle. Feeling overwhelmed by the sudden plunge from intense emotion back into ordinary things, she had to give vent to her feelings somehow and, leaning forward, she urged the horse into a gallop, keeping her seat with the expertise that naturally followed years of training and experience. Nigel caught her mood, at least in part, and he rose to the reckless challenge. The route over the stony track was losing its snowy covering. Riding Cass, he tore along with her as icy rain began to pelt their faces and a cold wind blew against their backs.

* * *

Maria might have been tempted to be angry and she knew Elis was furious with Nigel, but she had work to do and it was right for her to return. Nigel and Margaret, had they considered it at all, would have doubtless assumed Elis' other visitor, the young shepherd, was still there at the croft; they could not have guessed at the intimacy of the hour they disturbed.

The elation of the stormy gallop replaced any sense of grievance and by the time they crunched over the gravel before entering the stable yard, Maria was calmer. With Nigel's willing assistance, she cleaned the horses and ensured they were dry and well rugged-up. Tack was returned to the racks with a hasty wipe; it would be given further attention on the following day and Nigel promised to return and help. With new water buckets and full hay nets, Ed and Cass were settled in their stalls; lights were switched off, the outer door was swung shut and bolted, and stable work was complete.

Indoors, Maria hung her wet coat on a hook in the anteroom and shook off the soggy boots with great relief. She peeled off soaking wet socks, pushed her feet into a pair of indoor shoes and went to the stairs, to make her way up to the bathroom for a hot shower. She heard Nigel calling for Margaret when he entered the kitchen and when his wife came, crossly scolding because he was dripping all over the clean floor, he told her that Maria was a "game girl"!

A Realisation

Robert was frustrated when he couldn't find a favourite novel in the library. As she searched too, trying to help him, Maria came upon a battered album full of black and white photographs. She set it aside, continued hunting and eventually discovered the book Robert wanted. He examined it with relieved care, rearranging slipping leaves in the old volume. Maria asked for his permission to look at the photographs; it was granted and she sat down near the fire with the album on her knees.

Peter wanted to join in, so Maria made a space for him beside her, and they spent some minutes exclaiming over pictures of Robert when he was a handsome young man. There were many black-and-white photographs of a pretty, fair woman who was obviously Sarah. Many other people smiled or stared solemnly from the snap-shots.

Meanwhile, Robert's attention was caught by a television pro-gramme and he relaxed into deep cushions in his armchair, still clutching the novel tightly as if to ensure it wouldn't go missing again.

Peter turned again to his story books, which bore brilliantly detailed and quite terrifying depictions of wolves and witches on the battered sleeves of such classics as Little Red Riding Hood or Hansel and Gretel.

Maria tucked the photograph album under her arm and went to the kitchen, where Margaret, straightening up after sweeping crumbs from the floor, smiled at her, emptied into a bin the contents of the dustpan and stowed it away under the sink. She smoothed her apron, began to turn her attention to stacking containers in the refrigerator, then changed her mind. "I might leave those until tomorrow!" She untied the apron strings and removed it, before drawing up a kitchen chair to sit with Maria near the warmth of the Aga.

Maria opened the old book again, rustling the fragile sheets of tissue that protected each page full of photographs. "Look!" She pressed a fingertip on a picture which was slipping from its fastening of stuck-on corners torn with age, and asked a question. "Is that … I mean, are they *Elis and Ian?*"

"Those two schoolboys?" Margaret asked. "Yes, they are."

"They seemed to get along well, when Ian hurt his head!" Maria said. "So, why is the fact that they're pals hidden, for most of the time?"

"They do get on okay," agreed Margaret. She hesitated. "Well, now they do. There was a bit of a falling out once. I don't really know why no-one mentions their relationship, I suppose it's taken for granted." She mused in silence for a moment, before going on. "Yes, of course it is. Keeping their distance from each other for most of the time has just been something that happened over the years."

Margaret frowned over the photographs, bending over some blurred images.

"Were they best friends?" Maria assumed that by "relationship", Margaret meant friendship. In one of the pictures, the boys were dressed in matching sweaters; they had their arms around one another's shoulders and they were laughing. They looked happy and relaxed and despite the fact that Elis had by far the longest hair, they looked very much alike.

Margaret turned and regarded her in surprise before she realised the question was genuine. "Oh! Well now, if you aren't sure what the photos show you, imagine Elis now, minus the beard."

"Cousins? They're not *brothers,* are they?" Maria started to feel slightly unreal.

"Did you not spot their looks are similar?" answered Margaret. Robert entered the room in time to catch her words.

Remembering, Maria thought she had, just on one occasion. "*Something* happened in my mind once. I wondered what I was actually thinking. I didn't understand it, but that was when I saw Elis grin!"

"Maria!" Robert poured coffee into a gold-edged cup, then set it on a gold-and-white saucer. He spooned sugar, stirring carefully, before leaving the drink on the counter for a moment. He made his way across the kitchen, to stand beside her. He moved a few of the pictures around, easily slipping them from the old paper corners. "Look! They are *identical twins!*"

She was supplied with another photograph and leaned over it, battling confusion.

"It's actually even more complicated than that!" Nigel had joined them by this time. He was tying himself into a capacious apron belonging, no doubt, to Mrs Moss. He set about washing up a collection of cups and plates at the sink, clattering crockery. "The boys are the kind of twins who each seem to know what the other is thinking! They'll speak both at once when they are together and it's incredible how often they turn out to be saying exactly the same thing!"

"Mm," Margaret remembered something. "Nigel, you told me that when they were very small, they chattered in twin-speak, and no one could understand them! It sounded like nonsense, to everyone else!"

"It did!" Nigel agreed.

Maria needed their attention. "So, when Elis suddenly turned up to visit Ian after that awful fall ...?"

"Yes." Margaret nodded. "Now you're getting it! He knew something bad was up! *He* had a sore head, too!"

Later, while Amelia settled Peter in his cosy bed, Margaret finished tidying the kitchen. After a few minutes, she hung up the vast pinafore worn earlier by her husband; then, she went to her bedroom to change her clothes. Wearing lounging trousers and a dressing gown, she returned to the quiet kitchen, got wine from the refrigerator, took three glasses from a cupboard and set these items on the counter. After that, she went to find Maria. The young woman was wandering aimlessly from room to room, still carrying the single photograph with her. Margaret suggested a chat.

Bearing drinks and a collection of snacks, the women retired to Robert's comfortable downstairs study, where a glowing fire was collapsing into embers. Red velvet curtains hung in gathered loops at the icy window. Margaret and Maria pulled and released tapes to let the heavy material fall, covering the cold glass and sweeping the carpet beneath. They all sat together in lamplight.

Peter was fast asleep upstairs in his divan bed and now Amelia spun gently around on Robert's swivel chair, pushing herself with an elbow on the desktop when she slowed down.

Margaret and Maria made themselves comfortable in a pair of narrow easy chairs, stretching their legs before the freshly-stirred fire as flames began to leap again, and reaching for more wine when their glasses were empty, feeling the occasion called for it.

"You'll laugh about this, one day!" Amelia promised.

Maria was not so sure about that. "It's so strange that I didn't see it," she marvelled. "We even talked about them both, without managing to touch on the family connection?"

"I really thought you knew!" Margaret told her. "Don't you remember? Once, I said all the menfolk care for their animals. We were talking about Elis but I meant Ian and Robert too. The family, do you see?"

"Oh! I remember! I think I do, anyway." Enlightened, she

reviewed their conversation. "I was washing my hands. Did I hear you say something like that, just then? Something about *all of them?* I think I assumed you meant all farmers like Elis ... *all the shepherds up in the hills!*"

"Maria!" Amelia was confused. "You're muddling me up!"

"Sit still then, dear." Margaret seemed to think the spinning chair might have mixed up her thoughts even more.

Maria followed her own train of thought. "Ian had just taken Cass out straight after he was fed, not being very careful at all actually. I couldn't link him with Elis at the time; I just didn't realise you meant *these* menfolk!"

"Silly you!" Amelia was glad that part of the conversation was over. She topped up their wineglasses.

Maria, feeling weak, was about to take an unladylike mouthful of her drink. Instead, she dropped her hand, realising how easy it would be to make herself ill, with a headache. "I wonder if those horrors in the shop fancy Elis, the way they seem to really go for Ian?" she mused. There was a pause, before she went on with an afterthought. "I'm not being very kind!"

Margaret thought the shop assistants were unlikely to go after Elis. "He chooses not to enjoy his wealth," she said. "They wouldn't like that, so much!" She had an afterthought of her own. "No, they *are* horrors!"

"Amelia, did you know? Did you know the men are twins, not just brothers?"

"Identical, to boot!" put in Margaret, making it worse.

Amelia gave herself another spin. "I don't know," she said. "I think so. Actually, I'm not sure!" The wine had made her insouciant; she smiled, ate cheese crackers and twizzled on her seat until Margaret grumbled that she felt dizzy just from watching her.

"Even if he was triplets!" Amelia announced, with a fine disregard for logic as well as grammar. "It's Ian who ... well ..." She lost her train of thought but it was obvious that she didn't mind.

Clearly, the family links were not of importance to her. Her companions began to feel maddened and Margaret noticed a dangerous expression on Maria's face as she leaned into the back of her chair, frowning still at the picture she held.

"I was coping with the discovery that they're brothers. Then it turned out they're twins!" Maria held up the photograph again, turning it towards the lamp, as if to shed further light on the confusion she felt. "Whatever is the matter with me?"

"I think you have a *connection* with Elis," Amelia said wisely, in an about turn from her mischief. She went on. "He is like no-one else, to you!"

Maria tried to grasp this idea. "So, you might have known Ian and Elis were brothers, but you weren't interested? So much so, that you can't even really say whether you knew or not?"

"Because it didn't matter, to me!" Amelia admitted.

Margaret looked worried but she kept her head bent for the next few moments. She turned her hands palm downwards on her lap and studied her pink nail varnish.

Maria pursued her train of thought. "I didn't realise they were brothers, let alone twins, even though I talked to each of them, and even rode out with them at times ... and I'd swear I didn't know ..."

"Do you mind about all this, really?" Amelia wanted to know. "Does it matter, to *you?*"

Margaret looked up.

"I don't know why I would mind so dreadfully," Maria answered honestly. "Except to wonder at how strange I seem! You've barely met Elis, whereas I ..."

For an uncomfortable moment, Maria was reminded of the embarrassment she felt, when she tried to talk to Ian about the croft. However, Amelia and Margaret were kind listeners and she went on. "I do remember getting some sense of recognition, the first time I saw Elis smile at me. Perhaps it was because Ian smiles far more often. At that time, though, the main things about poor Ian's face were a shocking black eye and a swollen cheek. Even so, I feel stunned by the whole thing!"

She paused, but a new thought had occurred to her. "There is something else. Surely, Elis sounds more *Welsh*, compared with both Ian and Robert?"

Margaret considered this, before answering. "Well, that is true! Elis has never left the farms, whereas they have lived and travelled abroad. He has a strong accent compared with Nigel, too."

It was small comfort. Amelia could happily insist upon her fondness for Ian and dismiss his similarity to his brother, for whom she felt nothing at all, but Maria was conscious that there was a trickier reflection for herself. At last, it seemed she couldn't avoid confronting a big issue. She had a sense of connection with both the men but what was the exact nature of her liking for Elis? Could it be genuine? Was it a real affinity, considering something must have drawn her to his similarity to his twin brother?

* * *

Margaret sighed and heaved herself out of her armchair, declaring she would fall asleep there if she didn't move. She placed an arm around Amelia who, despite her words of wisdom, still looked pink in the face and somewhat excitable. Sensibly, she encouraged the younger woman to leave Maria on her own, saying they would go into the kitchen and make coffee.

Left behind in the peaceful room, Maria watched a little flame dancing across the coals in the hearth. At last, she set the photograph carefully on the mantlepiece and tore her gaze away from the faces of the two boys. She listened to the ponderous tick of a grandfather clock in the corner of the room, where a heavily-shaded lamp glowed and a collection of ancient books and ornaments lent an extra feeling of times-gone-by to the atmosphere.

Maria deliberated over Amelia's responses, considering they were anomalous with regard to two interesting histories that had come to light at the Manse. It seemed she did not care one bit that the men were twins, even though she was powerfully drawn to Ian. Amelia saw no romance in the life of that similar brother, living a solitary life away from the Manse. She wasn't interested in analysing her own reaction to Ian, saying only that she loved him.

And yet, her imagination was captured by Robert's tale of love, perhaps even infidelity, which happened long ago, when he was a young man! Why did Amelia let her mind linger over the story of the young gypsy? Was it because, as a pretty young woman herself, she could imagine being in the role of either Rose or Sarah?

Amelia loved Ian unequivocally and it was a fact she readily expressed. This led to a serious reflection for Maria, who brought herself to a point of truth and was ready to consider it. Unlike her friend, she knew both men personally. She saw traits in them which she admired, even loved. She could draw comparisons … if she so wished.

Maria began to send herself into deeper confusion as she tried to hear, inside her head, the voices of Elis and Ian. Elis, she knew this for sure, was gruff. He had a deep voice. Was Ian's voice (which was certainly touched with the same Welsh accent) lighter because his conversation and words were often light-hearted, she wondered? They had shared so many jokes, and so much laughter. In her conscious comparison of the two men and the discovery that she could in fact spot some similarities between them, Maria was beginning to take something of a risk with her emotions.

She thought about Ian's lively expression and the way his eyes gleamed with humour; then, she remembered how Elis looked at her with amusement when she expressed herself in schoolgirl's language. Honestly, she knew she enjoyed making Ian laugh, but she felt the same sneaking satisfaction when his brother relaxed and grinned about the shrew incident! There was something else about that, Maria thought. When Elis laughed, she was relieved. She was glad he could see the funny side of life sometimes.

* * *

"I wonder what their falling-out was all about?" Maria was scrubbing potatoes for baking.

"Who knows?" Amelia, incurious, thought it must have happened so long ago, it barely mattered at all. She waited, poised to prepare extra vegetables, leaning back against the counter near Maria with a sharp knife in her hand. "Anyway … who would dare to ask?"

Margaret brought a colander full of carrots from the larder and tipped them in a heap on a chopping board beside some green vegetables. With an automatic gesture she removed the pointed knife from Amelia's grasp, since it was being waved perilously near Maria's head. She set it down on the board while Amelia turned her attention to scraping and slicing a cabbage.

"We'll *never* know what upset them," Margaret stated placidly. She started to prepare her casserole, causing sizzling as cubes of raw beef and chunks of onion hit oil already heating in the frying pan. She pushed a wooden spoon into the mixture to turn the beef, and altered a dial on the hob, to lower the heat. "I don't think it was a row over a woman, since they always seemed to have different tastes!" She screwed the top of a pepper shaker, holding it over her pan, then added a pinch of sea salt and stirred the seasoned mixture well. "Hmm … that's not the best way to describe it! Different choices, perhaps. However, even Robert doesn't know anything about it," she mused. "Except that it happened."

"Different tastes …" If Margaret hesitated for a second after she said that, it was barely perceptible and neither of her listeners noticed that she actually glanced at Maria before she continued to speak; yet it was a comment that was to return to Maria's thoughts one day.

THE BALCONY

Shortly after the New Year began, there came a day of calm weather. Not only was there no sign of a storm, or threat of more snow and ice but the air was unusually mild. Thin sunlight shone against the windows of the house. Very early, Robert sent Peter running around to each of the occupants to ask them to assemble at his door at eleven o'clock that morning. (Peter was to be sure to tell them, it was a party!)

Both Maria and Amelia immediately sought out Margaret for her advice about what might be to come, and how best to conduct themselves. Were they to dress smartly? Was Robert's gathering a cocktail party, or perhaps for brunch? Were gifts in order? It was a good thing Margaret was on hand, to advise!

Robert was there, at exactly eleven o'clock, to admit his guests. He held the door ajar and announced, courteously: "Enter, troops! Ladies first!"

Ian looked well presented in brown trousers, a checked shirt and a tweed jacket with leather patches on the elbows. He had tan-coloured loafers on his feet and Maria could detect a whiff of the expensive cologne he favoured. She felt glad she had consulted with Margaret. It was apparent that running up to Robert's door wearing a pair of jeans and a sweater would have been dreadfully out of order! The occasion was important to the old man, and they needed

158

to be respectful.

Maria and Amelia had brushed their hair and put on some make-up. They wore skirts and neat tops from Maria's collection of clothes, and no-one knew Amelia's skirt was rolled over a few times at the waist. Peter was smart too, with his fringe flattened with a little water. Margaret, who was never lazy about her appearance, wore a tartan skirt and twinset, all in shades of fawn and burnt orange. With her short hair styled and sprayed, she looked very pretty.

Robert's suite was in an attractive part of the mansion. Windows overlooked parkland, and rooms were spacious. The master bed-room had a sizeable en suite bathroom and a tiny private study. This was Robert's second official study, where he kept his reference books and papers, with client records, all relevant to the counselling work which he occasionally still undertook in a private capacity.

A coal fire burned brightly and a heavy rug was thrown before it. With a careless disregard for its age and beauty, the dogs sprawled there. Having spotted a gathering and feeling hopeful of treats, they were already comfortably warming themselves. A massive tapestry hung against one wall, with a depiction of a hunting scene in muted colours. Maria was glad there had been no evidence of hunting around the house; no sad, stuffed trophies, no guns. It crossed her mind that she would not have made friends with a family who liked to shoot wild creatures.

Amelia liked the layout of the rooms. "At home, my office is my actual bedroom," she told them. "There are letters, bills, lists and all my diaries! All over the place!"

"No, no!" protested Robert. "You can't sleep well like that!" He opened French windows that led onto the balcony and there, on a round mosaic-topped table, were all the ingredients for making martinis.

Nigel and Ian pulled chairs into the room, collecting them from the other bedrooms and taking some out to place near the table.

Margaret declared she needed her thick jumper and trotted away to
fetch it from her room. They all spent a very sociable hour or two,
drinking martinis or sherry, sharing olives and salted nuts and chatting.

"If anyone is feeling cold," Robert announced, "there are piles of
well-aired blankets on the chest near my bed. Help yourselves!" He
assumed a cheery air of party-host and he was very happy. Dressed
in an ancient tweed suit and wearing a deerstalker hat, he urged his
guests to join him on the balcony.

Peter was supplied with juice in a plastic cup, and a packet of
crisps. He made a nest amongst the brilliantly-coloured cushions
on the king-sized bed, held his blue bear and before long, covered
with a fleecy throw, he fell blissfully asleep. Boy, cringing unnecessarily in case someone removed him, lay his feet.

Maria stood on the balcony, clasping her drink, admiring the
view. The parkland held many spots where she had ridden, sometimes at a walk, others, cantering along. She had taken the horses
over fallen logs sometimes, although the memory of Ian's fall was a
thought she hastily discarded. For the first time, she noticed that a
rose bush clung to the corner of a walled garden and a few early
buds were visible, glowing red amongst the leaves.

She had taken care of the horses especially early. They were exercised together, with Ed being led beside Cass, then groomed and
made comfortable. She was inclined to make the most of her freedom from the chilly outdoors that morning. She wandered into the
bedroom, where the rosy child slept with the dog nearby.

Maria patted Boy, and turned her attention to the pile of blankets. She chose a thick, blue one and wrapped it around her shoulders, then headed for a seat near the fire. Ian was there, stooping to
add a few chunks of coal with the fire tongs, and he looked up and
smiled.

"Alright, Maria? A spot of time out? You deserve it!"

Lately, Ian had seemed very quiet in comparison with his usual teasing self. Even though he smiled now, she thought his eyes looked a little shadowed. Maria knew he had felt somewhat disheartened by her determination to remain distant after his fall. For a moment, she wondered what he had on his mind. Many days had passed since she crossly told herself to stop her constant analysing of his behaviour!

"Yes. It is nice to have a rest!" She settled into a deep, easy chair and tightened her blanket around herself, absently fingering the silken edges.

Ian straightened and shifted the fire guard back into place. He let his gaze linger on her face. "You're looking pensive!" Unconsciously, he reflected her own thoughts about himself.

Maria hadn't spoken to Ian about her discovery of the photograph. He didn't know anything of her astonished response, or the conversations that followed. She guessed that no-one else had relayed them. After all, what was there to say? Ian had always been a twin! There was nothing for him to learn, so no personal comment seemed appropriate, especially as she would soon leave the Manse. There was a hum of conversation coming from the balcony, with occasional bursts of laughter; people were socialising, chatting casually.

"I think Ed and Cass were quite pleased to find themselves back in the stalls so soon," she told him. "It's time out for them, too! I might give them another quiet day, tomorrow ..." Feeling warm near the fire, she relaxed, with a sense of contentment overall. However, those dark eyes were now so familiar and the faintly serious air about Ian served to intensify that similarity to his brother. Her mind, so recently shocked, was not as peaceful as it might have been.

They chatted there by the hearth, inconsequential, keeping one another company in an easy way, as familiar friends do. Before long, Margaret and Amelia made their way, arm-in-arm, to the fireside, laughing and saying that was enough of the cold winter air, for now.

Ian went to refresh his glass and found Robert opening champagne. With a splash in a new glass for everyone and the drinks distributed, all his guests gathered together and the tall glass doors were closed.

Robert was holding a long-handled, silver spoon, which he had used to scoop olives from a jar. Now, he tapped it against his glass and called for the attention of all present.

"I shall begin this short speech with a quotation! As follows:

"Man loves company, even if it is only that of a small burning candle.

"Thank you all for coming! I'm glad to see you all together, for what must be one of our last gatherings as we near the first day of January and the New Year. I hope you are enjoying this sparkling morning, and the view of the park.

"When I look at that view each day, it always lifts my spirits, but I must say, these past few weeks have been especially happy. Ian and I, we rub along alright during the year. I am always delighted by the company of my brother and his dear wife. And this Christmas time, along came Maria, Amelia and Peter! It's been lovely.

"Maria, you have cared for my animals so well! Amelia, how musical you are my dear, and what a good mother, too.

"It won't be long until we disperse but until then, I wish you all a very Happy New Year and propose a toast to same!"

"Hear hear!" There was a general chorus of agreement and the toast was drunk.

A New Shock

There came a telephone call for Amelia and she went into Robert's study to receive it. It was good news! A representative from the local council explained that she could go to her house and would be able to open the front door and enter at last. A group of men from the village were helping all those who had been affected by the floods and Amelia would have a driver as well as a police escort, to keep her safe. She emerged from the study with pink eyes, and the strain of being separated from her home was evident now. She was determined to take advantage of this kind offer. She made haste to prepare for the car ride.

Peter wouldn't accompany his mother because the caller advised against taking a child into the damp lower rooms of Amelia's house. It would be a trip simply to take stock of the effects of the flooding, and collect possessions.

"I must go," Amelia told the others frankly. "I can at least pick up some of our things. I hope so, anyway, because if I wash and dry Peter's pants overnight once more, they will fall to pieces!" Of course, she promised to fetch Teddy, too.

The way was still hazardous and Amelia would be driven in a jeep and assisted over the last stretch of boggy ground. She would be able to spend a couple of hours checking over her home. Perhaps she could begin some cleaning; she hoped so. It would be sensible for her to return later and she would continue living at the Manse for the time being, at Robert's kind invitation.

Nigel and Margaret said they would take Peter for a long walk with the dogs, and afterwards they'd bake biscuits and he could have fun making shapes with the cutters.

Robert congratulated Amelia on this new development. Affected by the general sense of change, he then retired to the privacy of the small study on the lower floor of the mansion, where he intended to address a few outstanding pieces of paperwork. In fact, after some effort to sort and prioritise correspondence, he moved to an easy chair to settle by the coal fire burning in the grate. He stooped and rattled fire irons as he selected the miniature shovel, dug a couple of chunks of new coal from the nearby scuttle and stoked the fire, causing crackling. Then he prudently swept up a little scattered coal dust in the narrow hearth. With a wall radiator also warming the small space and a lamp offering its yellow glow to match the leaping flames in the fireplace, the room was very snug. The single, narrow window was shaded by an embroidered blind, its silken tassel hanging unused. Stretched out on a faded rug, the two dogs demonstrated their approval of their master's nap and all was peaceful.

When Margaret popped in with a cup of coffee for Robert before setting off on her walk, she found him very comfortable. She knew he felt tired after his small party, the day before. He rested his heels on a footstool and let his newspaper fall unread. He was glad of a peaceful day.

* * *

Maria had visited the horses very early as always; now, she returned to the stables to feed and settle them. She had already decided to let them continue to rest until the following day and they were content. Before long, thanks to her efforts, they were rustling fresh straw as they shifted and pulled at the filled hay nets in their stalls. Their coats, under light indoor rugs, were sleek from brushing and their long necks gleamed.

She went into the tack room and inspected the saddles, bridles and headcollars, which she was proud of keeping spotlessly clean and shining with saddle soap as well as elbow grease. She took a bridle from its peg and quickly cleaned the bit but there was little more to do just then. With the stable doors safely bolted, Maria could leave the animals and she went back towards the house, crunching in her boots over the strip of gravel beyond the stable yard.

When Maria re-entered the quiet house, she found herself with a welcome period of free time. She wandered into the kitchen and considered making a sandwich but her mind and body shared a condition of lassitude and she lacked appetite. She took a handful of peanuts from a silver dish near a fruit bowl in the centre of the long kitchen table, cracked a couple open and stood still while she ate them. Despite excusing herself and the horses from a ride, Maria's typical diligence in the stables had used up a couple of hours and it was now mid-morning. There was a new loaf on a wooden bread board near the Aga. She deliberated, then rejected the thought of eating anything more.

Forgetting, or not wanting to remember that abandoning a meal could lead to a headache for her sensitive system, Maria opened a cupboard and chose a glass, found an open bottle of white Merlot in the refrigerator, and poured a drink. Soon, carefully carrying her glass, she went up the tiny back staircase, opened the latched door, walked through the passage and then went on a few more paces to arrive at the door of her room.

She took a hot shower, washing away the familiar scents of horse and hay, replacing them with the sweetness of lily-of-the-valley selected from the box of gels and lotions given to her by Margaret. Soon, wearing a short, white towelling robe over a silk top and shorts, she wandered about the bedroom, barefoot on the opulent carpet. She brushed out her thick hair until it fell like a cloud about her shoulders. Then, feeling a little too warm, she shed the robe.

The combination of wine and a sense of freedom suddenly made Maria feel happy. She twirled on tiptoes, making her hair fly up and around her. Memories of childhood came unbidden, and she tried to move as she once did in dance classes, adopting a few ballet positions, circling until she felt dizzy.

Outside, the day was dry and still. Maria stood at a window, letting her head stop spinning, watching a couple of black and white magpies beneath the great oaks on the parkland for a moment. *Two for joy …* She remembered the old saying.

Maria knew the air outside was very cold. The thought made her shiver and she tugged at the cord that sent drapes swishing across the window. In the half-light, she contemplated taking a nap. Postponing the idea for the moment, she turned on the central light and when she caught sight of herself in a mirror, she paused to examine her reflection. Her hair shone fawn and gold. The silk garments gleamed, pale pink, white and cream. She rolled the dimmer switch to reduce the glare and her serious reflected face looked youthful, freckled and great-eyed.

Maria sprayed her shoulders with perfume and added deeper fragrance with rich moisturising cream on her hands and arms. She thought about Elis. In her self-indulgent mood she daydreamed. Those deep brown eyes! The fine hands and the way he touched her brow with gentle fingers … then her mouth. The thumb, pressing her lips … it reminded her … but the memory (if it *was* a memory) vanished, blurred by the effects of the wine, lost in her thoughts as they moved on.

She wondered. Did Elis care about *glamour?* She held her hands before her face, permitting vanity, admiring the gleam of champagne-coloured nail varnish. She finished her wine, reflecting that it seemed Amelia was right to be optimistic.

"Things could work out very well …"

There came an abrupt tap at her door.

Without pausing to consider who could be there, Maria rashly opened the door at once. It was Ian, also fresh from a shower. Post workout, he was casually clad in jogging bottoms and sandals. His torso was bare, except for a towel slung around his shoulders. He looked down at the young woman who stood, lightly clad, before him on her endless legs. The cascade of hair framed her face and the wonderful eyes met his. Like Maria, he had not thought twice before approaching her door and he had come to find her with the simple intention of asking if she had any objection to him taking Cass for a ride in the indoor school.

The question was forgotten. There was a sweet, pure scent in the room and Maria stood very still, in softly muted light. His expression intensified as, unsmiling, he held her gaze and his demeanour became deeply brooding.

Ian's familiar presence was overwhelming. Maria was still affected by the wine and her mind, already slipping dangerously into a powerful daydream, seemed to stray into an unreal world she couldn't control. She looked up and into fathomless brown eyes and her thoughts were in disarray. *Elis?*

"Maria …!" He spoke and no, her thoughts wouldn't be reined in. As if in an involuntary movement, she held out her arms. It was a dancer's gesture, a balletic movement, but it was what Ian had waited, so painfully, to see. With a step forward, he entered the room, shed the towel from his shoulders and with his right hand pushed the door, which closed behind him. The lock snapped shut.

Ian stooped, put his arms around Maria and spoke into the cloud of her fragrant hair. *"Oh God! You look … I can't …"*

Their human frailty, their youth and passion overtook them both, and there was no turning back.

* * *

Margaret took it upon herself to give the kitchen a thorough cleaning in preparation for handing it back to Mrs Moss. Amelia, seeing her assembling cloths, spray cans and antiseptic wipes, offered to help. "I like going round with these surface wipes!"

She busied herself for a few minutes, then observed that the return of the cook seemed to be an uncertain thing. However, Margaret was positive it would happen.

"She will be back; she often has a tantrum! Robert's too soft really."

"She won't like it that we reorganised a few things," commented Amelia.

"No. It doesn't matter though." Margaret was pragmatic. "She shouldn't have left poor Robert in the lurch, should she?"

Nigel took over some tasks when Amelia went to put Peter to bed. He rolled up his shirtsleeves and began to wash down cupboard fronts. Apropos of nothing, he mentioned that Elis had been absent as usual at Christmas but it was nice that he came to see his brother after the riding accident. "He was a bit miffed when I collected young Maria on the day of the storm!" Nigel was not blind! He had noticed the younger man's dark expression, after all.

"Maria could be about to become as elusive as he is," his wife told him. "He deserves a companion but he is lucky because Ian was smitten too, for a while."

"Ian and Maria had fun," said Nigel, remembering. "How they laughed!" He considered the events of December. "Two pretty, single women … but no fights!"

"Mm, in fact a real friendship I think," she answered.

"Even though they are different?" Nigel observed on a questioning note. "Maria is very strong!"

Margaret thought about the younger woman's own strengths. "They aren't so very different, in some ways. There was so much common sense in Amelia when she coped with Ian's nonsense. She never bothered to call him out when he teased Maria, just waited and held her tongue. Plus, there is wisdom in her mothering."

"Well, you're right!" Nigel agreed. "And Maria does seem to be wise, too."

"With absolute determination to leave luxury behind her and follow Elis, whom she loves!"

THE GROOM

Robert asked Maria to join him for a private chat in his study. With typical attention to detail, he told her what time she would find him there and she duly tapped on the door after the morning's stable duties were complete. When she entered, the dogs thumped their tails on the ground in welcome as they regarded her from their places on the rug and Robert, who was seated in his swivel chair, indicated a fireside seat for Maria and waited for her to take it. He turned to face her. "You can tell the dogs are used to you, when they don't leap up! You're part of their household now!"

"I love them!" Maria confessed. "I've enjoyed looking after them very much."

She knew this was to be a conversation about the return of the groom, Abe, and that her work with the horses and dogs was coming to an end. It was always the plan that Maria would leave soon after New Year, but it felt as if that time had come too fast and she was full of mixed feelings.

Robert explained that her full wage had been transferred into her bank account, and she thanked him. "Working here and sharing time with everyone over the past few weeks, has been one of the happiest and most interesting times I've ever had," Maria made sure to tell him honestly.

He hesitated, shuffling papers before looking her in the eyes with a measuring stare. "Well now … don't run off yet, my dear."

Maria wasn't sure what to say. "I mustn't get in Abe's way," was all she could think of, in terms of something that wouldn't lead to an awkward conversation. However, Robert must have decided to be direct.

"Go up to Shepherd's Lot, won't you? Before you decide what to do next."

Maria remembered his kindly forbearance when Elis bound up her bitten hand. She thought there must have been many things he guessed over the past weeks, considering he was a psychoanalyst and an experienced older person. Up until this point, he had not voiced a personal comment of this kind.

She returned his gaze, even though she was suddenly wondering how much awareness he really had.

"Sometimes," Robert said, "all the thoughts and feelings, even the actions we have undertaken, need to go behind us." He was silent for a moment. Watching his expression, Maria thought he looked a little tired, even sad. He continued in his old-fashioned way. "We have to make a decision, or a choice, and then act upon it. Thus, our actions speak louder than our words."

He stood up. Maria got to her feet too, and they shook hands formally. She thanked him, feeling genuinely grateful towards him. She knew the messages in his words must have been carefully considered.

* * *

Abe was a surprise to Maria since he was quite old, possibly close in age to Robert himself. She was present when he arrived, finishing her work with a feeling of determination that another groom would be unable to find any fault at all.

The horses pricked their ears and stared when the old man entered the stables, making for their stalls, offering pieces of carrot and whistling softly to them. Cass whickered in pleased recognition.

Abe looked around and nodded approvingly as he noted how clean and tidy everything was.

"We had lovely rides," Maria told him. He was content, the hunters looked well. Jaff and Boy wagged their tails, coming to lean against his legs for a fuss. He could not have been prouder of the welcome the animals all gave him if they were his own.

She took him on an inspection of the tack room, hoping he would not object to her changes. She decided to be direct, and explained that she really enjoyed polishing up the harness and irons. Again, he was impressed. "It had got away from me a bit," he admitted. "I'll keep it alright, now!"

With a touch of diffidence, she confided her plan to go up the croft now that she was free to leave the manse. She said she wanted to go alone.

"You can ride there," said the old man unexpectedly. "Take Ed. Then, just fix the bridle and stirrups, give him a bit of a slap and tell him to *go home!* I'll look out for him!"

"How ...?" Maria felt sure Ed would run off.

"Ed knows how to work in harness," Abe told her. "He will pull a light cart."

This was obtuse, Maria was not planning to travel in a cart!

"A hunter in *harness?*"

"Robert trained him when he was younger, and he loves it!"

What was the relevance to the horse's safe return to Abe? Maria did not want to be rude but she had to ask. "So ...?"

He continued to explain. "*So,* he understands voice commands!"

* * *

Maria left her luggage heaped up in the porch near the kitchen.

"You'll be back in Elis' jeep to collect those bags!" Margaret chose to be very honest, and Maria allowed herself an emotional leap of hope.

Everyone was gathered at the front of the house when she

emerged, riding, from the stable-yard to the side of the mansion. Ed's hooves crunched on the pebbles in the great driveway; aware and interested as a healthy horse should be, he raised his head in surprise upon seeing people there.

It was going to be very embarrassing if Elis would not let her stay! Maria dismounted, but she walked around the horse to stand on his right side, held his reins with one hand, and did not put her arms out towards anyone. Her friends each said goodbye in their own way.

Robert came up, and shook her by the hand, saying "thank you!" In her turn, Maria thanked him. When young Peter solemnly copied him and held out his own small hand, Maria grasped it, then crouched, to smile at him. "Thank you for helping me in the tack room!" she said.

Nigel gave her a bear hug which made her gasp. Margaret was crying and laughing both at the same time, dabbing her tears with a lace handkerchief; she followed her husband, and simply patted Maria's arm. Amelia and Ian came up together, to plant kisses, feather light, on her cheeks.

Maria could bear no more. She ducked beneath Ed's chin, grasped the looped reins in her left hand, and with a leg-up from Nigel she mounted Ed again. With his head turned towards the open space beyond the driveway, and the hills, he began to prance. Another glance at the group of dear friends ... and most were smiling. Amelia and her son stood hand-in-hand, but Ian had walked a short distance away from the group. He stood still, with his hands in his pockets. He watched Maria steady the horse and settle herself in the saddle. When her stirrup irons were satisfactory and she looked up, somehow, she caught his eye and saw the familiar grin appear on his handsome face.

She applied gentle pressure to the horse's sides with her calves; gladly he sprang forward, and they were off, cantering at once, scattering gravel. No-one but Ian could know the exact reason why

Maria was crying, but it didn't matter. She stood up in her stirrups, sent Ed into a gallop and left them all behind in seconds. In fact, they didn't witness how hard her tears flowed.

The morning was bright and cold, the ground had dried well and Maria urged the horse to race along. At length, knowing he would probably gallop home too, she slowed him down.

* * *

Maria rode on. When she went to her bed the night before and turned back the covers, there was a single, red rose lying on the cream cotton pillow. Now, she faced the truth as best she could.

She had toyed with the idea of blaming Ian for many events since she came to the Manse, and even for their ultimate fall from grace. Ian it was, who rode Cass, upset her and caused her to run out to the fields, where she met his brother. Ian came to her door on a darkening winter's afternoon, when she was thinking about that identical brother, dreaming of being complimented on her beauty, feeling romantic.

Yet, in reality both events were led by her own actions. She could have been philosophical and never lost her temper over the unplanned ride, then perhaps she would not have met Elis in a way that led to an interesting hour in his croft! Strong-willed as Maria was, she probably should never have told Ian he had to check with *her* before taking out one of his grandfather's own horses! Furthermore, it certainly was not Ian's fault that at last Maria, distanced from reality by wine and happiness, saw and responded to the powerful similarity, which he bore and she sensed, to his twin brother.

Maria recalled his serious face as he watched her preparing to leave and the way, when he saw her glance at him, he tried to smile in his typical way. The brothers were barely different from one another, she realised, even in terms of character. It was a fact that she would never know their reasons for distancing themselves from one another over the years, ending up cordial but not particularly close but, at a guess, the reasons must have been partly linked with their similarities. Perhaps, if they spent time together, they would have become obviously competitive. Maria would never be able to confide fully in anyone at all, but she was so determined to go to Elis, and so sure Ian would find solace in the company of Amelia, she thought she could face her future.

* * *

Ian and Maria remained together for some time after their passion was spent; entwined but relaxed, saying nothing at all, conscious of the drone of the central heating's mechanism, the occasional bang from elsewhere in the house as someone, returning, closed a door. Shadows lengthened in the warm, dimly-lit room, where they were safe from discovery with their privacy guarded by an automatic lock.

When Ian stirred, Maria remained amongst the pillows, lying with her eyes half-closed, drifting; her thoughts somehow cushioned by sleepiness and comfort. He raised himself on one elbow, to gaze down at her face.

Although she was not looking at Ian, she held one of his wrists, wrapped gently in slim fingers. He noticed there were freckles like the ones which smothered her face, dotted, delicately, over the backs of her hands. He bent his head to kiss the fingertips that lightly encircled his arm, then spoke in a voice full of emotion.

"I asked Amelia to marry me ..." It was a comment both ridiculous and inevitable.

For a heartbeat, Maria felt pain but swiftly it was overwhelmed by the truth. This was Ian speaking to her. Not Elis. She opened her eyes and let her hand slip from his wrist.

"I know ..."

"She said *yes*," he continued, still with an air of confession. For a moment, he lowered his head into both hands and sat very still. Then, he sighed and looked up.

Calmly, she turned her head on the pillow to focus glowing

grey-green eyes on his face.

"It will be fine. Because I am going to go and live with Elis ... for ever." It was a dramatic remark, said as a statement of fact and Ian already knew this, just as Maria had guessed he would marry Amelia. They understood one another.

They were silent once more, breathing quietly, holding their gaze. He sighed, and shifted but when he saw the freckles that outlined the curved bow of her lips, he caught himself before he fell again. With a heavy sigh, he sat up. Maria, deeply moved by his tenderness and the ardent demonstration of his longing, sat too, partially covered by the quilt but naked above it, unashamed in front of him.

He took the shawl that lay by her pillow, shook it out and gently folded it around her. He kissed her cheek softly. "I think ..."

Maria stopped him. "No ..." she said, not unkindly. "Don't tell me what you think."

Ian clothed himself, preparing to leave. To cover his shoulders, all he had was the fallen towel. Their eyes remained fixed on one another's face, until he stooped to put his arms around her, burying his lips in the fragrant coils of her hair, stifling the words he had wanted to say.

Almost imperceptibly, she leaned her head towards his mouth but she did not raise her arms to return the embrace; instead, clasping her shawl, she remained still and murmured one word.

"Enough."

* * *

Nothing had truly changed for Maria, who wanted to be with Elis.

Ian was likely to suffer the most. If Maria had chosen him instead of Elis, he would have fallen for her in every way. And yet, he also loved Amelia. He was capable of making a life with her, and being happy.

Would they live successfully from this point onwards? Maria with her chosen partner, Ian with a sweet lover who would become his wife, and whom he respected for her beauty and her musical gifts? Would they survive without agony, despite carrying a guilty secret? Time would tell.

However, Maria was absolutely resolved about something. She knew that Amelia (who once feared Maria cared for Ian) was now perfectly sure her real interest was in Elis, and this was true. As for Ian's feelings, Amelia knew he was merely flirting with Maria during the early days of her stay in Robert's household. If she began to fear things could change, that thought was abandoned as time went on. She had stopped imagining he might learn to love two women, in a similar version of that true history that had enthralled the old man's listeners. If Amelia had a worry when she asked Maria to talk once before, now she had developed faith in Ian and they must not spoil it.

* * *

It was barely midday but Robert felt very tired. Leaning on his walking stick, he made his way slowly through the great front entrance where the doors still stood open since he and his guests flooded out together just a short time earlier, to say their farewells to Maria. He had a sense of loss, and yet no reason to feel sad. Maria, he knew, had made up her mind to go to Elis, and if his grandson was as delighted as Robert expected him to be, then all would be well.

Amelia came to Robert's side to put a hand under his free elbow, while Peter skipped alongside his mother. They were both dear to the old man now. He believed they would stay, because that was what Ian wanted.

Margaret, also returning through the wide doorway, had watched the vibrant young woman leaving their little group, riding confidently and fast. She was reminded of mornings during the past few weeks, when she stood at the narrow window on the upper floor, polishing the glass, or carefully watering the hyacinths, and watched a pair of horses galloping over distant fields, and knew the riders were Ian and Maria.

Many thoughts flooded her mind, and she remembered ...

How Maria had coped in the early days of her stay at the Manse. Ian teased her, saying her beautiful hair was the colour of nuts. He flirted as was his custom, but found this strong woman knew how to rebuff him when she chose.

The way Maria was shocked by her own feelings, first when Ian galloped off on the horse who had been so lovingly stabled, then when he had let the dogs follow Cass, and they got exhausted. Maria even took to her bed that night, but she fought to understand the man and her role, and in fact (Margaret suspected), to protect him.

Ian's confession, when he sat by the Aga and accused Margaret of wearing her nurse's face, and said he would think about how he might be making Amelia feel. (He admitted, Maria would be his favourite, if she didn't beat him up.)

Margaret began to feel guilty. She paused at the foot of the stairs, and didn't continue on towards the kitchen. Nigel had turned to pull the doors closed behind everyone, and Ian was standing nearby. Nigel noticed his wife's hesitation. "Are you alright, my dear? She'll be fine, you know."

Nigel began to unfasten the front of his jacket, frowning down at the buttons. Ian remained silent, standing in the same spot a few feet away from his uncle.

"Are you going to get a drink with Nigel?" Margaret asked. "Lunch will be ready in an hour, if you need something to eat."

Ian gave Margaret a passing glance but he turned his head towards the doors, now closed and bolted as usual. "No thanks, Auntie Marg'. I'll go up to my study," he said in a low voice. "Or my bedroom ... maybe."

Margaret walked across the hall with her heels clicking on the polished floor. She went to stand close to her husband and together they watched Ian's retreating figure as, head bent, he went slowly up the staircase. He arrived at the first landing and they saw him raise a forearm to his face and draw his jacket sleeve across his eyes. Then, turning to climb the next set of steps, he was soon out of sight.

Nigel turned to Margaret, and his expression was thunderstruck. "You know what?" he asked.

"He's crying," she said in a low voice. "I know. Does he love two women? Is Maria the one he really wanted?"

"Oh …" Nigel put his arms around her. "Good Lord!"

Margaret wept a few tears of her own. "He told me!" Her voice was a whisper. "Weeks ago. He said, if only Maria didn't tell him off so much, it would be her. I thought he was fairly light-hearted about it. He sounded quite funny and I thought I knew what to say. I asked him to consider Amelia more carefully. I did it because I knew that Maria favoured Elis, even then."

She felt in her pocket for her handkerchief. It was already very damp. "I even thought that Ian might let them both go, so he could go back to the way he was before these times.

"I cried when Maria left, because I would miss her! I didn't know I was about to feel so sad for Ian. Perhaps I should have told him to hang on? Would he have been able to behave himself better? Could he have made Maria love him?"

"If that had happened, you'd probably start to grieve over Elis and his loss! I know it's tough, Margaret." Nigel was soothing. "I understand how sad you are … but look, you couldn't foretell the future! Of course not, and it doesn't matter. You gave sensible advice but people have hearts and they can't always control them, and Ian couldn't quite fit into the jigsaw pattern we all made this season.

"We can't change things for our nephews, neither one of them. These are grown adults and they will live their lives as they see fit, and sometimes we won't understand and that's no-one's fault."

HOME

At the croft, Maria dismounted, loosened the girth and led the horse to find the water tap near Ben's stable. She filled a clean bucket for Ed while Ben, with his head over the half-door, pricked his ears and watched with interest. She secured the reins so they would not dangle, slid stirrup irons up the leathers and checked and refastened the girth. She ran her fingers over the supple leather, which she had spent so much time carefully cleaning, patted Ed's neck and walked him to face the down-hill track. He seemed to understand what was about to happen, and threw up his head in excitement. Maria felt torn inside. It was almost impossible to part with this lovely animal, after he had been in her care for so many weeks. With faith in the old groom's instructions, now she forced herself to say *"go home!"*

There was no need to smack his rump; he knew exactly what to do. As soon as she stepped back, he cantered off, blowing excitedly through his nostrils and performing a couple of silly bucks before speeding up, just as she had suspected he would.

A bit disorientated after freeing her charge, Maria hesitated for a few seconds, then moved away from the track and stooped beneath an ash tree to gather a few early primroses. Holding her small posy, she walked over a strip of grass and arrived at the front door of the croft.

* * *

When Maria entered the cottage, where the front door opened immediately into the kitchen, everything was peaceful. A fire crackled as always, behind an old-fashioned wire guard. The white cat was sitting on the arm of an easy chair, with his tail curled neatly around his paws. He opened his pink mouth in a thin squeak of acknowledgement, then gave the fur on his chest a couple of licks with an air of finishing-off.

"Hello, Smoke." Maria stooped to remove her riding boots.

The cat stopped washing, stood up and stretched himself, before he leapt onto the stone floor. He rubbed his body against her calves, purring hard. Stroking his head, she glanced at a row of outdoor garments hung on iron hooks and saw the long, heavy coat was missing. She gave Smoke a final pat and went to the sink, where she held a striped cup under a tap to fill it with cold water and added her handful of primroses before placing it in the centre of the scrubbed wooden table.

She filled the small pan with water and set it on a gas hob to boil, then made coffee in a tall jug which she covered with its hinged lid. She placed it beside two mugs and a sugar bowl. After these preparations, she took a poker to the coals in the hearth and stirred the fire into a lively blaze. Thin, wintry sunshine filtered through a window and the room was cosy. Maria knelt on the rag rug before the fire, with the cat affectionately leaning against her as she unplaited her hair.

The door opened and Elis entered with his dogs pressing behind his legs. He grinned widely when he saw Maria. "Robert's horse galloped past me! I thought that might mean you were here!"

Jess and Seb' were tired and muddy. They drank from their water bowl, greeted Maria briefly with ducked heads and wagging tails, and flopped onto the rug. They accepted her presence as a matter of course.

Maria stood up, with the cascade of light brown hair tumbling over her shoulders and her grey-green eyes on Elis' face. There was laughter in her voice, as uncontrollable as his own happiness and the faintest air of defiance when she spoke. "I've come to stay!"

With a few long strides he stood before her, and took her into his arms. "You need to say it again," he murmured, holding her tightly. "What you do speaks so loudly that I cannot hear what you say!"

Then he lifted her face in cupped hands and kissed her, so hard she could not possibly have said it again, even if she tried.

Postscript

Two years slipped by. Abe arrived at the croft one morning with the sad news that Robert had passed away during the night.

At the funeral, Amelia wore black lace, a slip of a dress that hung in folds to her calves; with her fair curls loosely tied with velvet ribbon she looked a little fey but took the usual solicitous care of her son and the flossy-haired baby daughter she clasped in her arms.

Maria twisted her own long locks into a shining coil on top of her head and dressed in a neat black jacket and skirt, worn with a modest blouse.

The brothers shared the duty of pall bearing with two others; dressed in black and because Elis had taken it into his head to shave off his beard, they were identical.

Robert's son and daughter-in-law had made their home in New Zealand and were comfortably settled; the Manse passed to the twins therefore but Ian, after making amicable financial arrangements with his brother, decided to take Amelia, Peter and the baby and emigrate to New Zealand too. There was no reason at all for Elis and Maria not to make their home in the great house.

They remained childless but they were absorbed in each other, content with the work they created for themselves and very happy.

* * *

Not just a pretty face.
Idiomatic

Never wrestle with pigs. You both get dirty and the pig likes it.
George Bernard Shaw

A meal without wine is like a day without sunshine. Jean Anthelme
Brillat-Savarin

A rose by any other name would smell as sweet.
William Shakespeare (Romeo & Juliet)

It is not enough to be busy. So are the ants.
The question is: What are we busy about?
Henry David Thoreau

Man loves company - even if it is only that of a small burning candle.
George C Lichtenberg

One for sorrow
Two for joy
Three for a girl
Four for a boy
Five for silver
Six for gold
Seven for a secret never to be told.
Nursery Rhyme

What you do speaks so loudly that I cannot hear what you say.
Ralph Waldo Emerson

Review Requested:
We'd like to know if you enjoyed the book. Please consider leaving a review on the platform from which you purchased the book.